The Sheriff and the Psychic

Welcome to Renewal, Book One

Peggy Jaeger

Copyright

Contents

Dedication

To T.C.
The sister of my heart; my Nutri-sistah!
You make me laugh, you make me smile, you make me feel loved.
I am blessed to have you in my life.
~ Peg

Chapter One

"Well, look what the wind blew back our way." Harv Dickensen smiled when the door to the Sheriff's office opened. "Didn't expect you back for another week at least, Cal."

Caleb Blackbear, Sheriff of Renewal, Oklahoma, crossed the wooden floor, tossed his hat on the desk, and settled his long body into a chair. "Thought I'd come back early and make sure you were doing your job. Wouldn't do for one of my deputies to be found loafing off."

Harv's laugh came solidly from his belly, causing the ample area to ripple with merriment. "It's good to see you, Cal. How'd everything go in Wyoming?"

Cal scraped his hands through his straight, short-cropped, ebony hair, sighed, and leaned back in the chair, resting his feet on the desk. "As well as could be expected. It's tough on my grandfather. He swears he can hear my grandmother's voice in every room. I think he expects to see her pop around a corner one of these mornings like nothing has happened."

Harv sighed. "It's hard losing someone after so many years together. Sherry and me only been married a third of the time your grandparents were, and if something happened to her I don't know how I'd be able to go on."

Cal nodded. "Rose and the girls are staying on a few days more. That might help some. So, fill me in. Six weeks is a long time to be away from this desk. What's been happening?"

Leisurely, and embellishing on a few entertaining events that occurred in the town since the Sheriff's departure, Harv related everything he could remember. The deputy described two bar fights resulting in overnight stays in the jail for the brawlers; an emergency run in the squad to the county hospital when SueEllen Chase went into premature labor just when her husband left town on business; some adolescent high jinx at the middle school. Nothing out of the ordinary for the usually quiet town.

The phone rang, interrupting Harv's laughing diatribe concerning SueEllen's labor screams. "Sheriff's office. Yes, ma'am." He reached for a pencil and scribbled something on a pad. "I'll be right out ma'am...no, don't bother, and don't touch anything, okay? Yes, ma'am. Thank you."

"Problem?"

"Maybe. That was Mrs. Coeltrain. Seems she's found a dead cow at the ranch."

"Coeltrain?"

"Oh yeah, you haven't met her yet." Harv's smile broadened as he moved from behind the desk and checked his holstered gun. "Came about two weeks after you left. Friend of Mabel and Jake Adams. She's staying with them for a spell."

Cal squinted at his deputy. "Why are you smiling like that? The last time I saw that look you had a weekend off and planned a little get-away to Oklahoma City with Sherry."

The smile turned to a cheeky grin. "Now that you mention it, seems you owe me some time off seeing as I've been managing this place practically on my own for the past month."

One corner of Cal's mouth twitched. "I'll think about it. Now about this Mrs. Coeltrain?"

Harv considered the Sheriff with a thoughtful eye. "Why'n't you ride out with me and see for yourself? I'll even let you drive."

"What a pal," Cal said, his heavy lids half closing.

Fifteen minutes later they arrived at the Adam's property.

"Doesn't look like anyone's here," Cal said walking up the drive. He tried the door and found it unlocked.

"Mabel? Jake?"

Without warning, a huge golden Labrador bounded from around a corner of the building barking wildly. The officers drew back, the sheer size of the dog intimidating. Its bark was downright deafening.

"Solomon, *basta! Sedersi.*"

The dog grudgingly quieted and sat at their feet, tongue lolling to one side.

Both men turned to the woman who'd commanded the dog. Cal's breath audibly caught in the back of his throat.

She couldn't be real. No real woman looked like this. Hair the color of ripe acorns, a deep nut brown, all shine, and gloss. Shimmering waves of it cascaded down her back, free and enticing. Cal rubbed the tips of his fingers together in anticipation of touching the silky tendrils. His eyes roamed over skin the consistency of china silk, smooth and even, and knew it would feel like warm velvet. Neither tall nor short, all of her was packed into a thin and well-dressed body.

The intimate perusal stopped when Cal found her eyes. They were the color of flinted amber, dewdrop shaped, with little slivers of bright gold-flecked within the darker yellow. The rest of her face was as exotic as those eyes. A chestnut-colored mole peeked out from the right corner of her upper lip and Cal found himself momentarily wondering what it would taste like.

They stood, rooted, staring at one another for a mere two or three seconds, but to Caleb, time ceased.

"Thanks for heeling your dog, Mrs. Coeltrain," Harv said. "He sure is a big'un."

"But gentle, Deputy. Really." She smiled. "He wouldn't hurt anyone."

Her gaze flicked from the deputy back to Cal.

"This is our Sheriff, Caleb Blackbear, ma'am. Cal, Mrs. Silvestra Coeltrain."

When she extended her hand Cal noticed the long, graceful digits and saw the tiny, simple gold band on the ring finger of her left hand.

A lightning bolt shot straight through him, clocking every facet of his being when their hands met. Mentally checking the sensations, his face remained calm, an expression in total opposition to the feeling going on inside his body.

She slowly drew back her hand and then placed both of them in the pockets of her pants. "Sheriff. I've heard a lot about you from Mabel. It's a pleasure to finally meet you. I hope everything is well with your grandfather."

"My grandfather?"

"Yes. I understood your grandmother recently passed away. It must be difficult for him to lose her after so many years together."

Cal may have been hypnotized by her eyes, but *that* voice. It could hold him prisoner. Rich, thick, and sweet like honey, every word was a note of music.

Caught off balance by his thoughts, Cal quickly tried to recover. "Yes, it's been a trying time. But he's doing fine now."

"You called about a dead cow, ma'am?" Harv asked.

Turning, she nodded. "Around back, down by the creek. Solomon and I were out walking when we found her."

The dog barked.

"We'd better go have a look," Cal told them.

Silvestra led them, Solomon in tow, to the creek bank.

"There she is." Silvestra pointed.

"Stay here, ma'am," Harv said. The two men made their way down the ravine.

"Well, at least we know who she belongs to," Harv said after spotting the ranch brand on her flank.

Cal's gaze turned from the woman standing on the hill.

"You okay, Cal?"

"Fine."

The slightest of smiles tripped across the deputy's face as he closed his pad. "A beautiful woman, isn't she?"

Cal squinted. "Stunning. Why is she here?"

Harv shrugged. "Visiting is what Jake says. But if you ask me, I'm kinda guessing it's more than just a friendly little stay."

"What do you mean?"

"Well," he said, scratching behind his ear, "When she first arrived, she looked kinda peeked and a few pounds thinner. But anyone can gain weight with Mabel's good cooking."

Cal smiled and glanced back up the hill. "Doesn't look to me like there's enough weight on her still."

"That's what I mean. I think she was sick before coming out here. Not sick like having the flu, but something more involved. Jake mentioned something, glossed over it really, and I didn't want to pry. She's real easy to look at, I'm thinking."

"You won't get any argument from me."

Lazily, Cal's gaze traveled down the trim body. The quick, piercing stab of desire was a surprise. He'd never had such a strong, instantaneous attraction before. The way those gold flecks had burned brighter in her eyes was the proof she'd felt something, too.

"Come on. There's not much more we can do here."

"Cow belongs to the Bolton ranch," Harv told her when they came back up the ravine. "Mind if I use your phone to notify them?"

"Go right ahead. The front door's open."

To Cal, Harv added, "I'll call the DNR, too."

The deputy walked back towards the house, Solomon trailing behind.

Silvestra's gaze turned to the dead animal. "Is there anything I can do?"

Slowly, Caleb turned to face her.

Just what exactly is it about you, lady, that makes me feel so jittery inside?

"I don't think so," he said at length. "Nate Bolton will most likely have her removed."

"The Bolton ranch is on the property adjoining this, yes?"

Cal nodded.

"I remember Mabel mentioning the name. Do you think anything happened to the animal to cause it to die here?"

"Probably wandered off from the herd an'died. They do that sometimes. Know anything about cattle ranching?"

"No."

He nodded again.

"Is something wrong, Sheriff?"

"Ma'am?"

"Why the persistent scrutiny? Do I remind you of someone?"

It was a full moment before he spoke. Tipping back the tan Sheriff's hat, Cal placed his hands on his hips and smiled.

"No, ma'am." Cocking his head to one side, he added, "In all honesty, I've never seen anyone like you before in my whole life."

Her eyes widened to the size of quarters.

A burning blush crept up her cheekbones as she glared at him.

"Harv mentioned you were visiting."

"Yes."

"Where's home?'

"Boston."

That surprised him. "You don't sound like you're from Boston. No funny sounding 'a's' or misplaced 'r's.'" He accented the letters like a true Brahman.

"I'll take that as some form of compliment," she said, finally finding her voice again.

"Plan on staying long?"

"Indefinitely."

Cal nodded. "Your husband with you, too?"

He saw her hesitate a beat before replying. "My what?"

"Your husband." He reached out and lifted her left hand, tapping a finger to her wedding band.

Yanking back the hand, she said "No."

Cal's heart twirled as a sprig of hope bloomed at her answer. "Does he plan on coming out soon?"

Silvestra's delicate brows furrowed and Cal noticed the color in her cheeks deepen. Before she could answer they were interrupted by a bellowing call from up the hill as Mabel and Jake Adams trotted towards them, Solomon leading the way.

"Shy, darlin'. Cal. What's going on? We came home and saw the squad in the driveway," Mabel said, stopping in front of them.

Quickly and calmly, Cal explained about the cow.

Mabel's blue eyes crossed over Silvestra's face. Cal saw her generous mouth turn downward. "Shy, did you...?" She stopped, casting a furtive glance at the Sheriff.

Silvestra shook her head. "No. Solomon and I were out walking when we came upon it."

Cal couldn't figure out why the sigh Mabel expelled disturbed him so much.

"When we spotted Solomon, he began barking so furiously, we thought you might be hurt." Taking the younger woman's hands in her own, Mabel added, "All sorts of horrible things flew through my mind."

"There now, hon," Jake said, patting his wife's back. "The girl's fine, as you can see. Cal, good to have you back."

They shook hands, Cal's gaze staying rooted to Silvestra's face.

"Not exactly the nicest way for you two to meet," Jake continued, casually. "We've been telling Shy all about our town residents and our friends. Filling her in on the local folk."

"Shy?" Cal said, arching one eyebrow.

He saw the swift look of vexation cross her face. Mouth taut, she said, "It's a nickname."

Her eyes turn the color of smoke when she's angry, he thought, intrigued by her response.

"I think I'll go back up," Silvestra said, turning to her hostess. "I need a cup of tea. *Andiamo,* Solomon."

"Go right along, darlin'. We'll be up soon."

Mabel registered the close, inspecting stare Cal followed Silvestra with. Hooking her arm in his, she said, "She was quite shy as a child and mercilessly teased because of...it. The name stuck. She's a wonderful girl, but she still gets a little nervous around people sometimes."

"What language did she speak to the dog?"

Mabel laughed. "Italian. Her father is Italian and Shy was born in Italy. Lived there until she was four. Then they all moved back to the States."

"She's very lovely," Cal said, his eyes still following Silvestra's form.

"So, tell us how everything went in Wyoming," Mabel said.

Cal took one last perfunctory look at the animal by the creek. While they walked back to the house, he related his trip and the call Silvestra made barely an hour before.

Mabel clucked her tongue. "I hope this business hasn't upset her. She's so delicate right now. She needs to rest."

"Has she been ill?"

Cal saw Mabel shoot her husband a glance when he opened his mouth. Dutifully, he closed it.

"Not exactly ill, no, but going through some tough times. We've known her and her parents for years. I used to teach at the same university where her mother still does. We've watched Shy grow up and have always felt she's an adopted daughter. When she needed to get away for a while, we offered her the use of the guesthouse for as long as she needs it. Truthfully, I'm hoping she stays a good, long time."

"Will her husband be joining her?" Cal asked.

"Her husband? Goodness, no."

He saw her nervously glance back at the house. Why was her denial so emphatic?

"Look," Mabel pointed. "Here are the Boltons."

She trotted up to the Jeep as it pulled to a stop in front of Harv.

Cal watched as the couple greeted their neighbors while his Deputy filled Nate Bolton in on the discovery.

That done, Nate came to Cal, hand extended. "Good to have you back, Sheriff. "

"Thanks, Nate. Ethan. Pris," he added, tipping his hat to the statuesque young woman accompanying her father and brother.

"How was Wyoming?" she asked, coming to stand so close he could smell the overpowering perfume she routinely wore.

"Fine," he replied, his eyes darting towards the house.

"Let's unpack those groceries, Mabel, and leave these men to their business." Jake took his wife's arm and led her towards their truck.

"Strange thing about this cow," Nate said, scratching his chin. "You're sure it's one of mine?"

Harv nodded. "You're brand's on her."

"Any idea what happened?" Ethan asked, his eyes traveling from Sheriff to Deputy and back again.

"None. Mrs. Coeltrain was out walking and saw it lying by the creek," Harv told them.

"That the lady visiting here?"

"Yup."

"Saw her in the Post Office the other day. Fits into a pair of jeans like nobody's business." His smile was more leer than grin.

Cal's back stiffened at the description.

"Come on," Harv said. "I'll take you down to where the cow is."

While the deputy and the Bolton men walked round to the back of the house, Cal found himself alone with Priscilla.

"Well, now you're back," she said with a feline grin. "I've missed you. Did you miss me?"

Cal watched the pout form on Priscilla's lower lip and from the corner of one eye saw Silvestra come to a window holding a teacup. The nervous way her hand shook as she lifted the delicate porcelain to her lips disturbed him.

Priscilla turned to see what was distracting him and frowned at the woman standing at the window. Boldly, she moved into his line of sight. Lowering her eyelashes, she touched one well-manicured fingernail to his arm, tracing an invisible line back and forth on it. "Why don't you come around for supper tonight? Cayla will fix something special if she knows you're coming. You know how she loves to cook for you. Then," she added, "Maybe we can have some private time together afterward. Go for a ride or even a late swim."

Her voice lowered seductively, as she positioned her body closer, her breasts touching and tickling his arm.

Cal moved back, breaking the contact. "Pris, don't. I made it clear before I left it was over between us. I meant it."

The pout grew larger, and to Cal's mind, extremely unbecoming.

"I know you were miffed with me," she said, cocking her head to one side like an errant child. "I apologized."

Cal snorted and folded his arms across his chest. "Miffed doesn't begin to describe how I felt, Pris. I told you from the beginning I wasn't going to be any woman's prize. Now let's drop it and part friends."

"I don't want to be your friend, Cal." She moved closer and frowned when he withdrew further. "I want you back in my bed. I've missed you."

The needling whine in her voice began to aggravate him. He shifted and saw Silvestra had moved from the window.

"Pris, don't do this. You're embarrassing yourself. Like I said, it's over between us."

Priscilla Ann Bolton wasn't a woman used to being told *no*. With a defiant toss of her head, she sent ginger locks swirling about her shoulders. "You're the one who'll be embarrassed when you realize how foolish you're being. Don't think I'll take kindly to you begging to come back to me, 'cause I know you will. You'll be sorry when I'm otherwise occupied and no longer available. It'll serve you right, Caleb Blackbear." She took off in the direction of the creek.

Cal watched her saunter away. Pris was, he knew first hand, a spoiled and selfish woman, used to getting her own way. In the past she'd been an interesting preoccupation. But when he discovered her in bed with the local veterinarian, his preoccupation dissolved. She'd tried to blame the indiscretion on Cal's lack of attention, claiming he spent more time on Sheriffing duties than on her.

Tipping back his hat, he started walking toward the house when the radio went off in the squad.

"Sheriff, do you copy?"

Cal got in the car. "I'm here Pete. What's up?"

"Got a call about a two-car collision out by Coldecart Road and the highway exit. Is Harv with you?"

"Yeah. Give me the particulars and we'll head right out."

When Cal alighted from the car a few seconds later he spotted the Boltons and Harv coming back up the hill and informed the deputy of the radio call.

"I'll take care of the removal, Cal," Nate told him. "I'll call over to Denny's from my truck."

The Adams' came out of the house together.

"Everything okay?" Mabel asked. When Nate told her it was she said, "You and Glory must come for supper soon. We haven't had a little get-together in a long while."

"I'll check our schedules and have her get back to you."

"Good to have Cal back," Jake said, watching the squad car turn down the drive. "Harv's a good man, but he's not Cal."

"I agree. Did you invite him to supper, girl?" Nate asked his daughter.

"He said he was busy." Priscilla's eyes slanted as Silvestra come out of the house and over to them.

"You obviously didn't press him enough." To Silvestra Nate said, "Thank you, young lady, for calling about the cow. Sorry to have troubled you."

She graced him with a smile and a wave of her hand. "It was no trouble, Mr. Bolton. I'm sorry you lost her."

"Plenty others where she came from, thank the Lord. Our ranch is the biggest one for a hundred miles in any direction. And, it's Nate, by the way. I don't believe you've met my son or daughter."

"Ma'am." Ethan tipped his hat.

"It's a pleasure to meet you." Silvestra extended her hand to Priscilla.

"Charmed," the younger woman answered with a smile that never made it to her eyes. When their hands met, Silvestra's body froze. An image, sharp, but fleeting crossed in front of her. It was too quick to see clearly, but a sense of dread spat ominously through her system.

After the Boltons said their goodbyes and drove off, Jake put an arm around his guest's shoulders. "You okay?"

She nodded, suddenly chilled. Rubbing her hands up and down her arms didn't help ease the cold.

"You see something in Pris Bolton?" he asked.

Silvestra squinted and sighed. "It was too quick. But the feeling was strong. I haven't felt something that intense since..." she trailed off, not wanting to remember.

Husband and wife looked at each other over the girl's head.

"Let's go inside, darlin', and get some lunch. I'm famished and I'm sure you are too." Mabel took Silvestra's hand and led her back into the house.

Chapter Two

"Saw Nate Bolton last night at the *Redneck*," Harv said, feet up on the desk and crossed at the ankles. "He said the Vet's report concluded the cow died of natural causes. Just wandered off from the herd, laid down an'died."

Cal nodded, closed the file he'd been reading, and strolled over to the office door. It had been three days since Silvestra Coeltrain reported the animal.

Three days since he'd seen her.

He and Harv had been busy with police work, more so than usual, and Cal hadn't had a chance to call the Adams and find out a little more about their lovely guest. Thoughts of Silvestra occupied him more than once when he should have been concentrating on work. At night, behind closed eyes, her beautiful face would appear, all cool and clean and elegant.

Leaning against the doorjamb, arms crossed, Cal silently viewed the main street of Renewal.

"It's finally quieted down some," Harv said.

"For the moment."

Main Street at mid-day bustled with people running errands, doing bank business, shopping. Cal surveyed the street, pleased by the order he saw, the continuity. *Renewal* was *his* town, his responsibility, and like a father presiding over a large brood, he felt proud to serve her.

"You've been pretty quiet these past few days," Harv said. "Something on your mind you'd like to share, get off your chest, maybe?"

Cal turned, slanting a wary look at his deputy. He saw Harv's blue eyes, wide and trying so hard to be innocent, and had to give an inner chuckle. "For instance?"

"Oh, I don't know. Seems to me ever since we went out to the Adam's your mind's been preoccupied. Kinda like you had an itch you couldn't get to. You know? Restless."

Cal's eyes narrowed. "Oh really. I hadn't noticed."

Harv placed his feet firmly on the floor under his desk, folded his shaky hands on top of it. When the Sheriff gave a man *that* look, it was time to quit while you were ahead. "Just asking, Cal. That's all. You've been through a lot lately, what with your grandma's passing, and breaking up with Pris Bolton, and all. I'm just worried about -"

"You don't have to worry about me, Harv." He turned back to the street. "I'm fine."

As he stared off into the distance a lone biker turned on to Main Street. Cal's excellent vision recognized the lean, brown-haired rider at once. As the bicycle came closer into view, he found his heart picking up an unfamiliar rhythm; quickening.

She stopped outside Clark's grocery, leaned the bike against a post, and went in.

"Think I'll take a walk over to Clark's and get a root beer," Cal said, taking his hat off the rack. "Want one?"

Harv stared at him for a second. "No thanks, Sheriff."

The deputy rose from his chair a moment later and watched from the doorway as Cal sauntered over to the market. Scratching his shaking head he asked the empty office, "Now what in Sam Hill is going on?"

He spotted her the moment he walked into the market. A lifetime of honed tracker's instincts never failed as he saw her tucked behind one of the food aisles, holding a small basket. The Sheriff stood for a moment, just watching. Today, her chestnut-colored hair was pulled back in a high ponytail making the owner look all of fifteen years old. Seasoned, faded jeans that fit like a second skin made his mouth water. A cream-colored shirt tucked into the jeans, two buttons open at the neck gave him an unobstructed view of the line of Silvestra's throat and collarbone.

If possible, she was lovelier than Cal remembered. Skin, unlined and free of artifice had his fingers yearning to run up and down its softness.

When she picked up two cans, delicate brow furrowing, and bit her bottom lip, Cal's mouth watered with lust. The freight train that crashed into his mid-section when her tongue flicked across her lips almost did him in.

"Mornin' Cal," Bert Clark bellowed from behind the counter. "How's the Sheriffing business today?"

Collecting himself, Cal smiled. "Same as usual, Bert. Can't complain. How's Mary Louise doing?"

"Better. Much, actually. Doc Lynton says she'll be up and around within the week."

"That's good to hear. A broken leg's nothing to sneeze at."

Bert nodded. "What can I do for you today?"

"Just thought I'd grab a quick drink," Cal said, walking toward the cooler section. He spotted Silvestra close by the frozen foods.

Feigning surprise, he smiled and tipped his hat. "Mornin'."

"Sheriff." Silvestra inclined her head a fraction, briefly touching on his eyes.

"Nice day," he said.

"Lovely."

They stood silent for a few seconds, each pair of eyes locked onto the other's face.

"Stocking up on a few things?" he asked, glancing down at her basket.

Her eyes stayed glued to his face. "Yes. I forgot to give Mabel a list of things I needed the other day when she came into town."

He nodded and leaned against the freezer. "Speaking of the other day, Nate Bolton had his cow necropsied. Seems she did die of natural causes."

"Just as you suspected."

Bert Clark stood rooted at the counter, clandestinely watching them out of the corner of his eye as he pretended to count the change in the register. The store was practically alive with tension, all originating from the frozen foods section.

"Well, I've got to get this done and get back to work," Shy said.

"Here, I'll help you," Cal reached for the basket.

"Oh, don't trouble yourself. I can manage."

Smiling broadly, he said, "It's no trouble at all." For the briefest of seconds, their hands touched when he took the basket. The impact of heat meeting heat was overwhelming. "Besides, I've been coming here since I was a kid. I know where everything is, even the good stuff Bert hides from the kids. Now." He took the small list from her hand. "Teabags. They'll be over here."

Silvestra followed him around the store as he ticked off the items one by one and threw them into the basket.

"You sure don't eat much," he said, cocking an eyebrow. "I can see why you're such a little thing."

Because it came so quick and unexpectedly, her smile stopped Cal dead in his tracks.

Silvestra chuckled. "I don't need much. Mabel insists on feeding me enough every night for three people. These few things are just to get me through the day while I'm working."

Cal swallowed. Hard. The impact of her smile still sat squarely on him.

"Working? Mabel said you were here for a rest."

Silvestra's eyes widened and then clouded over. Her smile disappeared as she flicked her tongue over her lips again.

"I-I am," she stammered. "But I have a few things that can't wait."

"Such as...?"

Before Silvestra could reply they were interrupted by the frenzied arrival of two jet black heads bobbing up to Cal and screeching his name.

The Sheriff turned and immediately engulfed the two girls in his arms.

"How are my favorite ladies today?" he asked, giving each of them a swift peck on the head.

"Fine," they said simultaneously.

"When did you get back?"

"Late last night," one of them said.

"Ridiculously late last night," the other clarified.

"Girls, this is Mrs. Coeltrain. She's visiting with the Adams'. These are my nieces, Winter and Summer Marin."

Silvestra smiled at the two.

"Where's your mother?" Cal asked.

"She's coming," Winter said.

"She had to stop at the bank," her sister added, staring intently at Shy.

Cal noticed and asked, "Is something wrong, Sum?"

The girl blushed, dropped her eyes, and said, "No. I'm sorry."

"It's okay," Silvestra said softly.

With one corner of his mouth tipped upward, Cal said, "You seem to have that effect on people. They can't stop staring at you."

It was Silvestra's turn to blush at the compliment.

"Mrs. Coeltrain's from Boston," Cal told the girls.

"Really? We've never been there. We've never been *anywhere*, but Mom says maybe someday we can take a trip east. Summer loves American History. It's her *passion*. She's always giving us lectures on great American leaders and stuff they did. She's better than having a history book to study from."

Shy's gaze turned to the other girl whose lovely face reddened. "I'm not that fanatical about it," she said. "But I bet living in Boston is really great. You can visit all the historic sights any time you want." Sighing, she added, "I hope one day I can see the city."

"Well, when you do you'll have to come and visit me. I know all the best places to see and the greatest restaurants to eat in."

"Is it as beautiful and exciting as I've imagined?" Summer asked, brown eyes wide.

Shy nodded. "And busy, frenzied, and wonderfully historic."

"Hey! I've got it now," Winter snapped her fingers. "You're S.G. Coeltrain."

Silvestra nodded. "Guilty."

"That's why I was staring," Summer said. "I recognized you from the picture on the backs of your books. Only you're much prettier in person."

Smiling, Shy said, "Thank you. Those pictures never do anyone justice," she added, wrinkling her nose.

"Books?" Cal said. "You're a writer?"

"Sometimes," she responded, the blush returning. Before he could question her further, Silvestra said, "I've really got to be going. I have a ton of work left on my desk. Thanks for your help, Sheriff. Girls, it was nice meeting you. I hope I see you again while I'm here."

With a last lingering look at Cal, Silvestra walked over to the counter with her basket. The girls, who hadn't seen their favorite uncle in a few days, held him captive where they stood.

In a low voice, Winter asked, "Didn't you know who she was, Uncle Cal?"

"No. Should I have?"

"Win, he's not going to read her stuff," Summer said, shaking her head. "It's for girls our age, not grown-ups."

"That's true." Turning to her uncle, she said, "Mrs. Coeltrain writes this totally cool mystery series for girls that takes place in the nineteen fifties. Kind of after Nancy Drew, time-wise. Sum and I have read all her books."

"All? How many are there?"

"What do you think, Sum, twenty, twenty-one?'

"Closer to thirty, I think."

Cal whistled.

He watched Silvestra walk out of the store, holding the small grocery bag tightly. She turned and smiled once at them and then left, almost colliding with the dark-haired woman who entered at the same time.

"There you are," the woman called, coming towards them. "Harv told us you were here," she said, offering her cheek for a kiss. "I sent the girls to search you out. How are things?"

Cal smiled at his younger sister, grabbing her for a hug.

Rose Marin resembled her brother in height, coloring, and bearing. There, the similarity ended. While Cal was quiet and thoughtful, steeped in introspection, Rose was outgoing, gregarious, and made a point of being physical, touching most people at least once when she spoke to them.

The girls interrupted what he'd been about to say by telling their mother about Silvestra.

"And she's beautiful, Mom, so much more than the photo on her book covers," Winter said.

"*And* she's nice. She invited us to come and visit her if we ever get to Boston," Summer added.

"Did she now?" Rose asked, scrutinizing her brother's face.

Knowing Rose was sensitive to every aspect of his makeup, Cal tried to hide the light he knew danced in his eyes from seeing Silvestra.

"Come on," he said, wrapping an arm around his sister's shoulders. "I think I'd like to buy you ladies some lunch as a welcome back to town."

"And I think we'll let you," his sister responded. "Then, you can tell us more about this fascinating visitor."

The eyes that looked so much like his own, lit with playfulness.

Chapter Three

Silvestra leaned back against the rock, content, her bare feet flirting with the water's edge. Faded, blue denim shorts, old and soft as velvet, and a *Boston* t-shirt covered her frame. She'd haphazardly top-knotted her hair, some disobedient tendrils falling in disarray around her ears and neck.

It's a perfect day. Perfect for everything but work.

She'd tried writing for a while but the warmth of the sunshine filtering through the windows was pleasantly distracting, almost as much as thoughts about a certain Sheriff were.

The sudden and intense fascination Silvestra experienced from that first day was as alien a response as she could imagine. But this pull, this internal trawl toward Caleb Blackbear was strong and forceful, and no matter how hard she tried, it wouldn't disappear. He was, undeniably, handsome, with his raven eyes and hair and that rugged physique. The surname told her he was of native descent and the distinctive high cheekbones confirmed it. When they'd shaken hands, the power springing from his touch was unexpected. Solid and total warmth spread through her system, and along with the heat, a spark of distinct control that intrigued her.

From Mabel, Silvestra learned Caleb was born to an Irish mother and Apache father. Racial prejudice followed them most of their lives until the burden and weight of it destroyed the family. Cal's father was killed during a knife fight in a county bar, his mother of a broken heart a scant year later. Cal was nineteen, his sister Rose sixteen when left without their parent's protection, they'd been forced to fend for themselves.

Mabel spoke with a great deal of pride when she'd told how the young man won a scholarship to college and worked two jobs so his sister could attend a private boarding school. The concentrated focus Silvestra viewed in the Sheriff's eyes, in the way he carried his body, showed he bore the sadness of life the way he would carry any other load: carefully concealed, denying public knowledge of any inner turmoil.

They were alike in that regard.

Silvestra sighed and loosened her grip on the pole, planting it between some rocks between her feet. Eyes closed, head leaning back on the rocks, she let her mind clear and drift. The sun was a soothing antidote to fretful thoughts, calming, and with a warmth slowly steeping through her system.

Suddenly, the line went taut. The pole began to bounce back and forth. Silvestra's eyes flew open, and with a determined stance, expertly reeled the fish in. Mouth set in a determined line, eyes focused on the water, she played with the line at first, letting the fish have some slack, giving it a false sense of hope.

A quick flick of her wrists and she effortlessly pulled the catch in.

While she took it from the hook, the man she'd been daydreaming about stepped forward from the trees. "They teach you to fish like that in Boston?"

"Italy," she said, dropping the fish into a cooler.

While she rebaited, he asked, "Italy?"

"I learned to fish there when I was a child. My father taught me." Silvestra tried to keep her hands steady as she easily placed the worm on the metal hook. She'd known he was standing at the edge, watching. Pulse quickening, Shy tried to remain calm, a difficult thing to do when the Sheriff was at a distance. Now, as he came closer, her stomach and legs began to quiver.

"He did a good job," he said, as he watched her cast the line again. "You fish like you were born to it."

"Thanks."

"You're not working today."

"It's too nice outside to be cooped up."

"I agree. It was quiet at the station, so I decided to ride around for a while."

"Mabel and Jake have been telling me for years how wonderful this place is," she said, leaning back on the rock. "How relaxing, how easy the pace is. I can see why they love it here. It's so peaceful. Even the water is clean and clear. I can see the fish swimming about."

"I don't suppose you can see much of anything in Boston Harbor."

Silvestra laughed again. "On a good day you can see some garbage. But no, it's not as clean and pure as this."

Cal leaned back on one elbow. "When my sister and I were kids, we used to skip school on nice days like this and go swimming."

"I'm sure your parents loved that."

He shrugged. "They didn't know. Or if they did, they never let on."

"Weren't you afraid of getting in trouble, or of missing stuff in school? Missing out on things?"

When he shrugged again Silvestra watched his black eyes harden as he glanced out over the water. "No. Rose and I were both good students, so it was easy to make up what we missed. Besides, we weren't exactly the most popular kids in school. There wasn't a lot for us to miss socially."

"It must have been hard to be perceived as different when you weren't."

He turned his eyes from the water. "Perception had nothing to do with it. In the eyes of most of the others, we *were* different."

Silvestra related, having experienced derision for most of her life from people who didn't understand and wouldn't take the time to learn about her.

She sighed. "I can imagine you were teased, cruelly at times. Children can be the most brutal creatures on earth when they want to. Everything is black and white, no grays for them."

"You sound like you know what you're talking about."

"I've been teased a few times myself."

And more than just teased.

"Kids never stop to see what's on the inside. They only see what's exterior. The coating, my mother calls it."

"Funny, my mother used to say the same thing. She'd tell Rose and me to develop thick skins, to realize people spoke out of ignorance because they were -"

"Jealous of you, of what you have, of who you are. Fill in the blanks."

They both laughed.

"Seems like our mothers could be cut from the same cloth."

She nodded. "Mabel told me yours was Irish."

"Yeah."

"So's mine. Really Irish," she said, rolling her eyes theatrically. "Born and bred in Dublin."

"And your father's Italian."

Her eyebrows rose. "Yes. How did you know?"

"You speak Italian to your dog, your middle name's Geo which I think is also your maiden name, and you learned to fish in Italy," he said, ticking each item off on his fingers.

"Very good deductive reasoning, Sheriff. I'm impressed."

Smiling, he raised his head and winked an eye against the sun. "Don't be. Mabel told me about the dog, and Winter and Summer both filled me in on your literary talents, hence the name Geo."

Silvestra's laugh bounced off the water. "And you're honest, too. An admirable quality in a lawman. *Oh.*"

The line came loose, the fish on the other end, running for its life with the bait.

"Got another one," he said.

"Oh, he's big. Look at him pull, how fast he goes."

She stood to get better footing while she stopped the line from casting. The effort from the fighting fish jerked her forward.

"Easy." His arms came around from behind to meet her hands on the pole.

"I can do it." The fish pulled harder. "Oh!"

"Sure you can," he answered, yanking back on the rod with her. "Now, let him go slack for a second and then reel him in."

"I know how to do this, Sheriff."

"Humor me." His hands closed over hers. With a sudden snap, he pulled the pole all the way back, making Silvestra fall back against him.

"Now, reel him in fast. Don't give him a chance to get off."

Drawing the line back into the spool, Silvestra didn't know which emotion was stronger: the excitement of catching such a generously sized fish, or the delicious feeling of Cal's arms around her waist, steady and firm. Leaning against his chest as they fought the fish, she discovered a rock-hard torso. He smelled of the outdoors, fresh and woodsy. Her legs wobbled, her stomach shook, and her senses whirled at the feel, and strength of him.

"Here he comes," Cal said.

They pulled the catch in.

"Got yourself a beauty, there," he said. "That'll be dinner for all three of you tonight, with some to spare."

"Oh, he's gorgeous," Shy squealed in delight. Holding the prize up to eye level, she evaluated the fish. The fight to catch him was worth the effort. Looking up into Cal's eyes, her smile froze in place.

Craving, pure and simple, vital and fundamental, laced through his gaze. Silvestra stopped breathing when she realized the raw need facing her. All too quickly, his eyes changed; softened; *smoldered*. Slowly, his head came down. Without thought, Silvestra leaned forward, rising on her toes. Cals strong arms pulled her closer. She went willingly.

The kiss was a whisper of longing, scarcely touching lips to lips.

Silvestra lost all sense of time and space. As brief as the kiss was, it shot through her like a rocket taking off.

Cal pulled back, his eyes locked onto her face.

"Congratulations," he said. "That was a fine job."

Silvestra nodded, her cheeks scalding. "I guess I should thank you. You helped."

"You can show your thanks by having dinner with me."

Surprise cascaded through her,

"Not tonight, of course. Mabel'll want to fry that fellow up right away. Another time."

Silvestra swallowed. "I-I don't think that's a good idea."

That lopsided smile had her regretting the words instantly.

"What's the matter? Afraid being seen with me will spoil your reputation?"

"What?"

He shrugged. "Old and bad joke. Look, I'm not asking you to ride and rope a steer. Just out for a nice meal together. That's all."

"That's all?" she asked. The memory of what she'd seen in his eyes, felt in his embrace, was fresh.

Cal tugged on her pole. "Yeah, that's all. Now come on. Let's get this guy unhooked and home to your hostess. He's got a frying pan with his name carved on it."

Silvestra surrendered the pole and watched him effortlessly remove the catch.

"I'm assuming you're done for the day," he said, tossing the fish into the cooler. "I would be if I'd been lucky enough to catch a beauty this size."

"Why? Wouldn't want to press your luck?" She tried desperately to keep the grin bubbling up inside off her face.

"Astute guess."

"Ah, that's where we're different then," she answered, taking the pole back. She rebaited and then cast the line into the water. "I know luck has nothing to do with it."

"What does?"

"Skill. Pure and simple skill."

His laugh rang through the trees and then swiftly silenced as the line started to bob.

The smile Shy flashed him was plain with raw glee and a stab of conceit.

"I don't believe this." Cal watched her reel the fish in. "I've been fishing in this creek most of my life and I've never caught anything as quickly as that."

"I told you," Silvestra teased, neatly pulling the fish from the hook. "Skill. Now," she added, rinsing her hands in the creek, "I think that's enough for today."

Drying her hands on the seat of her shorts, Silvestra picked up her cooler and pole. Slipping into her sandals, she said, "I'll have to do this more often. I'd forgotten how much fun it can be.

Squinting at her, Cal barred her path through the trees. Hands on his hips, head cocked to one side, he asked, "Think you're pretty slick, don't ya."

She heard the sportive mockery and met it head-on. "Skilled, Sheriff. Skilled."

For the life of him, Cal couldn't figure out how she'd caught the fish so effortlessly.

It was almost like she knew it was there.

With the sun haloing her head from behind, Cal felt the need to touch her again barrel through him. Leaning in to do so, he saw Silvestra's color change from a healthy, rosy glow, to chalk. The pole and cooler tumbled to the ground.

"*Silvestra.*" He yanked her hands, found them like twin blocks of ice. Suddenly remembering what Harv told him about her health, he asked, "What's wrong? Silvestra, are you all right?"

She stared up at him, a lost expression crossing her pale face. Brows corrugated, the line between her eyes thinning, she shook her head and said, "Y-yes. I'm...I'm okay."

The color took its time coming back to her cheeks.

"Are you sure? You went awfully pale for a second." When he felt some of the warmth begin to return to her hands, Cal instinctively rubbed them with his own, cradling her fingers and palms.

After blinking a few times, Silvestra said, "I'm fine. Really."

Cal didn't believe her. "Come on, I'll walk you home." He took the pole and cooler in one hand, the other still holding hers, and began leading them down the path.

They were silent for much of the walk back.

She's even more fragile than she looks. Whatever illness or accident brought her here is still obviously a part of her.

He'd never seen anyone go dead white so quick before.

And her hands.

Ice cubes were warmer.

Mabel met them at the door to the house. "I saw you walking up. Harv called. Says he needs to tell you something and your cell wasn't working. Wants you to call him back."

He excused himself and pulled his phone from its waist clip.

When Cal came into the kitchen a few minutes later, he told Mabel what happened.

"That happens to her sometimes," she said with a nod. "She's usually very tired after. I made her go lie down."

Cal sighed. "I've got to get back. Tell her..." He shook his head. "Just tell her I said goodbye, will you?"

"She told me to say thanks for your help."

"I didn't do much," he said, remembering Silvestra's finesse. "Hope she's feeling better soon."

"She'll be fine," Mabel assured him.

But would she?

Chapter Four

The stinging started in her nail beds, and like lightning, shot upward. Leaning back in the chair, she lifted her fingers from the keyboard. The burning turned to a cold, wet, numbing. Behind closed eyes, she gave the vision, cloudy at best, time to take shape.

Green hues dominated. Iris colored one moment, holly-hued the next. Through the haze, she heard a sound, familiar and yet not. A call, distinct and heart-wrenching, for help. Not a human voice. It was too deep, too guttural to be human. An animal, maybe. But what kind?

The clouds shifted. A clearing surrounded by what looked like a forest materialized. Thick, rich grass shot up, tall and strong, from fertile soil. The sweet smell of chlorophyll was potent. Suddenly, her eyes began to burn. The clouds dispersed, flashes of sunlight prevailed.

Then she saw it, almost buried in the thick turf.

The animal's mid-section rose and fell rapidly, heaving, the breathing labored and hard. The call sounded again, a lonely foghorn with no shoreline in sight. The animal's nostrils flared, the massive, bulging, red tongue sagging to one side. There was a branding mark on the flank, plain and legible.

A freezing chill iced through her. Death, final and bleak, solidified through her senses.

The scene began to shift, dimming. The fog once again engulfed her senses.

Abruptly, all went black. The animal, the meadow, the trees, ceased to exist.

Silvestra opened her eyes and stared down at her hands. They were cold, the nail beds cyanotic. Flexing them a few times, trying to get the blood back into them, she sighed heavily.

A great weariness swallowed her whole, but she refused to succumb to its strength. Getting up from the chair on legs shaky with fatigue, she moved to the phone. Hesitating only once, she forced herself to dial.

It has to be done. I have no choice.

Cal drove with a reckless speed he couldn't put a name to.

When Silvestra called, her voice so tired, so fatigued, a spear of passion, razor-sharp, ripped through to his soul. He had to get to her. Fast.

Throwing the car into park, he tore from it in one brisk motion. Jake met him at the opened front door.

"Come on in, Cal. Shy's in the den with Mabel."

"Is she all right?" he asked, removing his hat. "When she called, I thought something happened to one of you."

Jake ran a hand through his thick salt and pepper hair and sighed. "No, we're fine. But Shy's, well, she's a little out of it right now. Always gets that way after..."

"After what?"

The older man stared up at the Sheriff and shook his head. "Think I'll let her tell you."

They entered a spacious wood-paneled room. Cal's eyes immediately were drawn to the petite figure lying across an oversized floral couch. Seeing how pale and languid she was, formed a lump in his throat.

"Cal," Mabel said, with a small smile. "Thanks for coming. Here's the Sheriff now, darlin'. Tell him what happened."

When Silvestra turned towards him, his heart stopped. A deep line of worry was etched into her delicate forehead. The elegantly shaped hands he'd held in his own just hours before were trembling. The dictates of his job were pushed from his mind. All he could think about was gathering her up into his arms, and holding her until all the worry, all the dread washed away. An unfamiliar feeling shot through him like a bullet.

Protection.

He wanted to protect this woman, shelter and shield this wonderfully desirable woman, for the rest of his life.

Silvestra tried to sit up. The effort looked almost too much for her.

Crouching next to the couch, Cal cradled one of her hands in his and said, "Why don't you just lie here and tell me what happened, Silvestra.

Dull eyes looked up at him.

Taking a deep breath, she began. "I was working down at the guest house. Suddenly, my hands started to go numb. That's the way it usually starts, with a tingling in my hands."

"The way what starts?" he asked, rubbing icy knuckles with the pads of his fingers.

Hesitating for a moment, lips trembling, she swallowed.

"It's okay, Shy," Mabel said. "Cal will understand."

Silvestra stared up at him. "My visions. I can see...things...in my mind. Things...other people can't."

He stared at her for a moment, his eyes briefly widening. "Go on."

"When my hands go cold like that, I know something is going to come to me. I can't fight the visions, they're too powerful. They come whether I want them to or not. I sat back and let this one come. That's when I saw the cow."

"The Bolton cow? The dead one?"

Chestnut-colored waves shook around her head. "No, another one. Similar, but different. The brand on the flank read *CR*. A large curlicue C with the R inside the opening."

"That's the Cambdon ranch, out by Winchester," Cal said. "Was the cow alive or dead?"

Running her tongue over her lips she said, "Dying. I watched it take its last breath."

"Here, darlin' have some of this." Mabel gave her a glass filled with an icy liquid.

"What does this mean?" Cal asked after she'd taken a large draft. "Is this something that's happened, will happen, what?"

"The cow is dead, of that I'm sure. And I don't think it died like the Bolton one."

Cal kept his face calm as years of law training had taught him. "How then?"

"The feeling is hazy, but I don't sense it was a natural death. And there might have been another one with it. I can't be sure. Everything went dark before I could see more, but I think I can describe where it was. The area's very distinctive."

"Go ahead." He took out a small notepad and began jotting down what she told him, her voice breaking once from fatigue. Cal stopped writing, gave the glass back to her, prodding her to drink.

"I know that place. It's part of the Cambdon ranch," he said. "Out on the back border of the property."

Standing, Cal addressed Jake. "I'll swing out there right now and see what's up."

"I'm going with you," Silvestra said, rising from the couch.

"That isn't necessary."

When she set her lips into a thin, firm line, he was at once enticed and angered. The stubborn tilt of her square chin made Cal's mouth water. He wanted to trace his lips down and around its edge.

"Shy's done stuff like this before, Cal," Jake said. "Helped police with investigations and such. She's used to seeing unpleasant things if that's what's worrying you."

Cal remained silent, staring at Silvestra. Even as she pulled herself up off the couch, he could see how unsteady and wobbly her legs were.

"It's true, Cal," Mabel said. "And she might be able to help."

He continued to stare, silently weighing their words. Silvestra squared her small shoulders and for a second he felt a sense of pride at the unyielding caste in her yellow eyes. Then, the Sheriff saw something else, something he'd not noticed previously: strength.

"You can come. But when we get there, keep out of the way. Understand?"

Silvestra nodded.

In the squad, Cal radioed his position and destination.

Silvestra, outwardly composed now, was anything but. Her head still reeled from the vision, an after-effect she hadn't felt in some time.

Over a year, she thought. I haven't had a vision this strong in almost a year. First, that ominous feeling with the Bolton girl, then that one by the creek. Now, this.

She shook her head and silently watched the road before them.

"What kind of police investigations?" he asked.

Silvestra startled at the harsh sound of his voice. "Missing persons. Children, mostly."

"What do you do, find them?"

"Sometimes. Usually, I can get a feel or a read of where the person has recently been. At times, though, I've been lucky enough to actually *see* where they are."

He nodded. "Ever work on any famous cases?"

Her heart skipped a few beats. The air in the car became stifling. Willing herself not to lose control, Silvestra pushed the remote on the door and lowered the window. "One or two."

They drove for a few more minutes until he asked, "Have you always been able to do that? See things, I mean."

She sighed; deep and long.

"Yes. Always as far back as I can remember."

"It must have been hard on you to have such a gift as a kid."

"It wasn't easy," she admitted, after a second.

"No, I don't imagine it was. Tell me about it."

"Seriously?"

"Yeah. I'd like to know."

Stunned, she ran her tongue over dry lips and silently debated. Cal's sincerity impressed her, as had his acceptance of her abilities as a psychic. Staring back out the window, she said, "I don't remember a lot when I was little, but my parents have told me some. When I was three and my grandmother died, was the first time they knew I had a gift."

"What happened?"

"She'd been for a visit, barely gone a week. My mother said I was looking at a family picture of all of us one morning and I started crying. I asked why Nonna looked so sad and why she was lying on her kitchen floor. My mother grabbed my hands, found they were like ice, and called my father. He told her to call my grandmother just to assure that she was okay."

Silvestra stopped and stared down at her hands.

"She wasn't, was she?"

"No. The maid found her as I'd described. She'd died instantly of a massive heart attack. Never been sick a day in her life. After that, my parents realized I could sense and see things other people couldn't. It was fun at times. I could always find lost items. When I got a little older, well...it wasn't as much fun anymore."

"What happened?"

Her eyes misted for a second, then just as quickly, Silvestra willed herself to stop. It was a long time ago, she told herself. The memory shouldn't still hurt so much.

"Silvestra?"

She shook the feeling off. "I'm sorry. I was remembering how sad it all was."

"Tell me."

The melancholy sigh underscored her feelings. "I was in third grade. We were supposed to go on a field trip to the Museum of Art. The night before, I had a vision of an accident. I told my parents and they kept me home for the day. They tried to warn my teacher and my classmates."

"Tried?"

She shook her head. "No one believed me. My parents never made my gift public knowledge, never told the teachers or anyone in the school. None of them would believe me about the accident. The Principal told my mother I was a highly strung and nervous child, and I was probably saying this to get attention."

"Christ."

"Off my class went while I stayed home. Never in my life have I wished so hard to be wrong about a vision."

"But you weren't?"

"No. The bus careened over a divider after it was struck, head-on, by a truck. My teacher, the bus driver, and three of the kids in the front of the bus died. The rest were all pretty badly banged up. After that, my parents took me out of school and had me tutored at home."

"Why? Don't tell me anyone blamed you for what happened?"

"No, not blamed. But there were...incidents...things were said and done. One group of kids routinely called me a witch whenever they saw me. My grades dropped and I began to have panic attacks when I had to go to school. That's when I started seeing a psychiatrist. That's when I met Paul."

"Paul?"

Silvestra stared down at her hands, twisting the wedding band around her finger. "My husband."

His mouth flattened, what she took for anger wafting from him. With a nod, he told her to continue.

"I did better at home in the long run," she continued. "By the time I was ready for high school, I'd come to terms with my abilities. The opinions of others didn't matter as much. I learned to accept it as a gift from God."

"You grew up."

Yes, she thought. I did. It was amazing he was able to put it so simply.

"My grandmother had a gift like yours," Cal said after a moment. "She knew when someone was going to die, what sex a baby was going to be. Things like that."

Silvestra turned to him again and studied his face. When it broke into a broad, boyish grin, a thousand butterflies flew about in her stomach.

"She especially knew who always stole her cookies off the window sill after she'd put them there to cool."

Shy's own smile came easily. "I don't think having second sight had anything to do with that."

He took his eyes off the road for a moment, his gaze doing a quick dip to her mouth.

"You know, when you smile, that little mole dances up your face just begging to be kissed."

Silvestra lowered her eyes and bit down on her bottom lip. For the second time since she'd met him, his frank complement unnerved her. The deep breath Cal hauled in could have been her own.

"You have a rather frank way of speaking, Sheriff."

"I can't be the first man to tell you how attractive you are, Silvestra. If I am, I'm afraid there are a lot of blind men on the east coast."

The challenge she saw in those ebony eyes, the craving so boldly sketched there, caused her heart to flip. "I'm just not used to men flirting with me."

His mouth formed a hard line. "I'm not flirting with you, Silvestra, be assured of that. Flirtation is much too frivolous a word for what I have in my mind."

She saw a muscle under his right eye begin to twitch

His words knocked the breath from her.

"Here we are," he said a moment later.

They drove through a broad iron fence painted black and parted in the middle. The top of the gates read *CAMBDON RANCH,* the letters forged into the iron.

Cal circled the car around the spacious, sprawling two-story home, to the office located at the back. Stopping the car, he quickly crossed to the passenger side to open the door for Silvestra and extended his hand, helping her out.

They walked towards the office together, Cal's hand protectively placed at the small of her back. She found the sensation both unsettling and strangely comforting.

When he knocked on the door Cal was bid a hearty entry.

"Blackbear. I haven't seen you for a dog's age."

The man who rose from behind the well-worn oak desk was roughly the same size and age as the Sheriff. Where one was dark, the other was fair, with sandy-colored, longish hair falling below his ears, and a ruddy complexion that told of many hours spent outdoors.

"How ya doing, Ben?"

The two shook hands, Ben's eyes drawn to Silvestra.

Cal's hand immediately flew to its resting position at her back. "Ben Cambdon, this is Silvestra Coeltrain. She's visiting with the Adam's."

"Nice to meet you," he said, taking her outstretched hand, eyes lingering on her face. Turning back to Cal after a few moments he asked, "What brings you and this lovely lady out our way?"

Cal's quick glance warned Silvestra to let him do the talking. "I was wondering if you were missing any cattle or have had any unexpected animal deaths or wanderings?"

Ben's blue eyes narrowed. "How'd you know about that? Casey just called in and reported it about ten minutes ago. I just got off the phone with Randall Denny."

"A cow down?"

"No. Three. Out in the back pasture. Why?"

Cal ignored the question, asking instead, "Mind if I ride out and have a look?"

Ben shook his head. "No, not at all. I was just gonna go myself. But I wish you'd tell me what this is all about."

"After I have a look."

Silently, Ben Cambdon got his hat and the trio walked out of the office.

"I'll take my Jeep."

Cal nodded and helped Silvestra back to the car.

"He's concerned about how you know," she said as they sped down the dirt road. "Why didn't you tell him?"

"No need to at the moment. Let's see what this is all about first."

A few minutes later they reached a fork.

"We have to get out from here and walk," he told her. "Do you want to wait in the squad?"

Silvestra shook her head and the three of them headed for the clearing.

When they came out of the small wooded area, Silvestra spotted two ranch hands squatting in the near distance. A short ways off to the right another young man stood, hands fisted on his trim hips.

As they approached, Silvestra's heart quickened. This was the scene set in her mind. The bright colors, the vivid textures, the smell of death lingering in the air.

The animal, now stiff with rigor, flies swarming around its mouth and tail, lay as she'd envisioned. The cold, brutal reality of death, so raw and so concrete caused viscous bile to bubble up in her throat. Squelching the queasy feeling, Silvestra mentally berated herself for the momentary weakness. A veteran of many a crime scene, she'd witnessed the aftermath of bloody brutality, and she'd thought herself hardened to anything. Now, she refused to get sick in front of these men, one in particular. For some reason, she feared his ridicule. With another mental shake and a deep, silent cleansing breath, Silvestra walked closer to the men.

"Ben," one of them said. "Sheriff," he added with a long look at the woman with them.

"What's going on, Casey?" Ben squatted down, one hand over his mouth as he inspected the animal.

"Don't know. We had a few stray off this morning, figured they'd be down this way. The grass is richer here than down back." His eyes shot over Silvestra before he continued. "Anyway, we were rounding them up, noticed a few were missing, and Kenny decided to head down, knowing he'd probably find them munching like crazy."

"Kenny?" Cal said, addressing the young man with Casey.

A visible Adam's apple bobbed nervously as the young man, no older than nineteen, Silvestra thought, said, "It sure is strange, Sheriff. All three of them stone-cold dead. This one here and then those two over by Zeke. Weird to have three go at one time, don't you think?"

Ben's eyes looked hard at his ranch hand. Rising up quickly, he faced Cal. "I think so, too, Cal. Now, what the hell is all this about? You knew about this when you got to my office. How?"

"Take it easy, Ben. Let's go check out the other two and then maybe I can explain."

Cal led Silvestra away from the questioning gazes of the ranch hands, one hand encircling her upper arm. His voice low, he asked, "Is this what you saw?"

"Exactly."

"Okay. Let's get a look at the others."

Ten minutes later, after Cal questioned each of the hands, he pulled Ben to the side.

Silvestra watched as the two spoke and noticed that more than once Ben Cambdon's eyes turned her way. The ranch owner gestured wildly, Cal his antithesis of calm. The smooth and composed way the Sheriff conducted himself and the business at hand impressed her.

Large hands placed in the back pockets of his pants, hat tipped back just slightly, Silvestra saw him nod and answer all of Ben's questions placatingly.

Abruptly, Cal tipped his hat to Cambdon and strode back to her.

"Let's go," he said, taking her arm. "I'll drive you home. There's not much I can do here."

In the car, she asked, "What is he going to do?"

"Well, Rand Denny's already been notified. He's the local large animal vet. Ben'll request a necropsy. Hopefully, it'll explain why they died."

"Do you think something was done deliberately to them?" she asked, crossing her arms in front, and giving voice to the notion nagging through her.

"Hard to say. It's mighty unusual all three died at the same time in the same spot. But there was no outward sign anyone messed with them. Hides were intact; no bullet or knife wounds on any of them."

"Their deaths just don't seem natural to me."

"We'll have to wait and see what Denny finds."

"What did you tell Cambdon about me? I caught him glancing over at me when you two were talking."

Cal felt oddly touched by the small note of insecurity in her voice. Up until now, Silvestra seemed the kind of woman who knew her own mind. She'd admitted the opinions of others no longer concerned her. But hearing that twinge of uncertainty in the question, he realized she *was* worried about what people thought of her.

"I didn't tell him anything about you being psychic if that's what you want to know."

"How did you explain why you drove out to the ranch?"

"I didn't, exactly."

"Why did he keep staring at me, then?"

Cal cocked a crooked smile. "Probably because you're real easy on the eyes. In case you didn't notice, the other men in that pasture had some difficulty keeping their eyes off of you, too."

Her cheeks grew scarlet and Cal once again noticed a characteristic gesture of her shyness: she bit her bottom lip and lowered her eyes. It was strange she was so unassuming about her looks. Skin as soft and perfect as a rose petal was rare, and Cal's fingers ached to touch so unique and extraordinary a creation.

They drove in silence for a while.

Cal silently berated himself again for his candor and reminded himself she was a married woman.

But hell, his heart countered. If she's married, where's her husband? And why would he let her come halfway across the United States without him?

The sweet scent of roses floating about her enthralled him. Perfume or shampoo, he wondered. Wafting through the sweetness was her own natural fragrance, light yet deeply sensual. He'd privately acknowledged the stares she'd caused at the Cambdon ranch irritated him. They were so openly lustful, so wantonly needy. And yet, she hadn't seen them for what they were.

Could a woman be so guileless, so unknowing of the effect she had on a man? Could this woman sitting beside him not know what she did to him, the passions just a look his way conjured up?

"You can let me off down at the guesthouse," she said when they turned onto the road leading to the house. "I think I'll rest a while before Mabel feeds me silly again."

When he opened the car door, she took his extended hand.

"Would you like to come in for something to drink?"

He nodded, slowly. "Thanks. I could use something cold about now."

Together, they went into the house.

From out of nowhere, Solomon bounded, barked once at his mistress, then Cal, and jumped on Silvestra.

"Solomon, *basta*," she laughed as the dog showered her face with licks. "*Ti amo, Solomon. Ti amo.*" The words quieted and soothed the animal.

"Lemonade okay?" she asked, crossing to the kitchen.

"Sounds great."

While Silvestra took down glasses from a cabinet, Cal petted the dog and afforded himself a closer inspection of the guesthouse.

The walls were a bright white with sheer eyelet curtains covering the windows. The living room had a small striped love seat and rocking chair, a table with an antique hurricane lamp, and an old oak upright piano in one corner. Next to the instrument was a workbench doubling as a table with a small computer, screen, and keyboard.

"My nieces were very impressed at meeting you," Cal said, remembering what the girls had told him. "I believe you're their favorite author."

He heard the ice tinkle into the glasses.

"I was impressed myself with the number of books you've written."

Perusing the quarters, Cal's eyes found one lone photograph atop the fireplace mantle. Crossing to it, he found Silvestra, smiling widely, her eyes dancing to some unknown merriment, along with a small boy of about four or five and an older man with graying hair. A rainbow-colored hot air balloon, grounded, sat in the distance. Cal picked up the frame and peered deeply at the three people. The boy bore a remarkable resemblance to Silvestra. The hair tint, the color, and shape of the eyes, even the smile were all hers.

"They're sweet. I'm glad they enjoy the books, they're fun to write. Here you go, Sheriff," she said, coming up behind him, the glass outstretched.

He nodded his thanks and took a long draught of the tart liquid. "More than enjoy. They hinted since I know you maybe I could wrangle an autograph. The way Winter put it was 'all our friends would just die of pea-green envy if we had a real, honest to goodness, S.G.Coeltrain autograph.'"

The color that rose instantly to her cheeks knocked the wind from him.

"I'll see what I can do."

The moment stilled. Cal couldn't take his eyes from her face. Everything about it was perfect, from the way the small, loose tendrils of hair dangled about her cheeks, to the mole that peeked out from her mouth. A rocket exploded in Cal's blood when he watched her nervously lick her lips.

"Your family?" he asked, holding out the frame.

Silvestra took the photograph and lingered over it for a second. Cal noticed the subtle tremor he'd seen before when she gingerly placed it back on the mantle. "My husband and son."

Cal hid his surprise at the age of the man she called husband. He had to be a good twenty years older.

"The boy favors you."

The smile was quick, and yet, he saw the sadness floating in her eyes along with it.

"Yes. Actually, in this picture he looks unbelievably like my father did as a child. I have a photograph at home of my father when he was the same age as Giovanni. The resemblance is extraordinary."

"Giovanni? Unusual name. But then, so is Silvestra."

"It's the Italian form of John. My father's name also. Giovanni Geo."

Cal stared at her, watching the way her fingers laced and unlaced while she spoke. He wanted desperately to take them in his own, rub them, soothe away the nerves displayed within them.

"Fine looking family you make," he said after a moment. Then, unable to stop himself, he added, "Hard for me to imagine a man being away from a wife who looks like you for any amount of time."

There it was again, that veil crossing over her eyes. What is it? What is she hiding?

He stepped closer and was encouraged when she didn't retreat. The memory of their all too brief kiss was still implanted in his mind, on his lips. Cal needed to know if the pleasure he'd felt before had been real or an illusion. "If you were my wife, I couldn't stand to have you away from me even for a moment. Why does he allow it?"

"Allow it?" Golden sparks suddenly shot from her eyes. "I'm not a slave, Sheriff, nor am I your wife. I don't appreciate -"

With a will of its own, his outstretched hand ran up one arm, causing her speech to halt.

Their eyes stayed locked as he ignored her words. "And why is it every time I get close to you I have this incredible urge to touch you, to feel your skin against mine?" His other hand followed suit up the opposite arm until he circled both of them with his massive hands. Gently pulling her closer to him, their bodies were within a whisper of touching.

His gaze roamed over her face, memorizing every facet, every angle. "I haven't been able to think of much else but you these past few days," he murmured. His fingers cupped her chin, tilting her head to meet his gaze. "What is it about you holding me prisoner, Silvestra? Makes me forget everything but you? I thought at first it was your eyes. That you'd hypnotized me. Those flecks of gold shooting out to the edges could tantalize any man. But it's more than that, more than your beauty." His voice was soft, worshipful, as his fingers trailed down and across the line of her jaw, up to her mouth, stopping at the little imperfection he'd been dreaming about kissing. Bending his head down, he added, "I've been wanting to do this for days. I've been imagining it. Envisioning it."

This was surely madness, he told himself. But he had to know if what he'd tasted at the creek was as appetizing and delectable as he remembered.

"You've bewitched me, Silvestra Coeltrain," Cal whispered. "It's as if I've known and dreamed about you always. Even your name sounds like magic."

He couldn't stop, didn't want to, and wouldn't if he could have. This woman, this enchanting woman was in his arms, warm and pleasing to his touch, like an angel sprung from his imagination.

Beneath his hands, Cal could feel how truly real she was.

Just when he would have claimed her mouth for his own, the searing screech of his cell phone parted them.

With an oath, he pulled the device from his belt.

Silvestra straddled her hands on the top of the love seat back, her attention focused on him as he made his call.

While he listened, Cal saw panic cross her face, read the alarm at what had almost happened. Silently he cursed himself for pushing.

"I have to go," he said.

She nodded, eyes round saucers, wet and glistening.

"Silvestra." He moved toward her.

The outstretched hand stopped him dead. "No," she cried, her voice shaky, unsteady. "Just...just go. This can't be. I...shouldn't have allowed this to happen...shouldn't."

The pleading expression in her eyes threw a twisting dagger into his heart. When tears pooled in the outer corners, something inside him broke.

His mouth set into a hard line, his jaw tensed as anger steeped through his system. In the next moment, he was able to curb his raging emotions.

Grabbing his hat, Cal raked one last look across her face. "You're wrong, Silvestra. Dead wrong. If I didn't have to leave I'd prove it to you. We'll be together like this again. We both know it."

Only after the engine gunned, spinning the car down the driveway, did he allow himself to breathe again.

Chapter Five

"Now, I won't take no for an answer. You're going and that's all there is to that."

Silvestra lowered her fork after Mabel made her announcement and took a deep breath. "But, I don't want to go."

"Too bad," the older woman clucked as she refilled her husband's water glass. "A good old-fashioned barn dance is exactly what you need to get you out of this funk you've been in for the past few days. See people your own age, have some fun. Laugh again. You need to get out and be with folks."

"But I'm with you and Jake. That's enough for me."

"Nonsense. While Jake and I are fabulous company and wonderful conversationalists," she threw a grin at her husband, "we're not exactly the same age as you."

Silvestra bit her lip to keep the smile threatening to explode from forming. "So? I've been with people my own age. I prefer spending my time with you two."

Placing the water pitcher down on the sideboard, Mabel resumed her seat at the table. "I think that's a compliment."

Shy smiled.

The older woman reached across the table and took Silvestra's hand. "Darlin', what I'm going to say is hard. Hard on me and most likely harder on you. I know how difficult this past year has been since the accident."

Silvestra's smile dissolved.

"No, don't do that," Mabel said. "I've watched you seal off the pain, deny the hurt. It isn't good to keep everything bottled up inside of you like this. Do you honestly think we don't hear you screaming at night when the dreams come?"

They sat silently for a moment.

"I've wanted to rush down to you every time, but Jake always held me back, arguing you have to deal with this by yourself. Well, as true as it may be, I can't sit around any longer and watch you waste away emotionally. When your mother called and asked if you could spend some time with us, I jumped at the chance to see you again."

"We both did," Jake put in.

"We love having you here. When you first came out you told us you needed time. Time to heal, time to think, time to work. Well, you've had your time and I still see the hurt in your eyes every time I look at you. I can hear the pain in your voice when you speak to your parents on the phone. You've been brooding, darlin', and enough's enough. It's been over a year now. It's time to take your life back. You need to be out with people. You're too young to lock yourself away forever."

Silvestra tried to strangle the sob that formed in her throat, but it did no good. Mabel turned and gathered her into her arms. "Go ahead and cry, darlin'. Despite what those expert psychiatrists think, crying does a world of good."

The tears came freely.

"Sometimes I miss them so much I can hear my heart breaking," she sobbed. "Then there are whole days that go by and I don't think of them with sadness. I only remember the happiness. Why can't it be like that all the time?"

Mabel ran a hand down Silvestra's hair. "If I knew the answer I'd bottle it and make a million. You're healing, darlin' and like all wounds, some days you heal faster than others. But sitting around brooding does no good. You know I'm right."

Silvestra stared into the woman's old and wise eyes.

Blowing her nose into a handkerchief that Jake so conveniently had handy, Silvestra nodded.

"All right. I'll go."

As the smile of triumph overtook Mabel's face, Shy added, "But I won't guarantee I'll have a good time."

"Honey, there are no guarantees in life," Jake said, helping himself to another biscuit. "But it can't hurt to try."

Silvestra took one last look at herself in the bedroom mirror and sighed.

At Mabel's coercion, she'd agreed to attend the dance. For two days she'd banished it from her mind, allotting as much time as possible to completing her latest book and expending much of her energy into forgetting about Caleb Blackbear. The manuscript had been sent off to her editor just that morning, and with nothing else pressing, came the realization the night of the dance had arrived.

Shy surveyed herself again. The simple denim short-sleeved dress Mabel gave her as a present was accented by a red and white checkerboard kerchief woven tightly and secured around her neck with a gold clasp. The waist was cinched with a matching belt. Running a hand down the expanse from waist to thigh, Shy realized just how much weight she'd lost over the past year. Mabel's cooking had put some of the flesh back on her bones, but Silvestra knew she still looked waif-like and too thin for her frame. Sighing, she continued her perusal. The boots she'd brought from home went perfectly with the outfit. Silvestra wanted to wear her hair tucked up but changed her mind at the last minute, deciding to wear it down, allowing only a thin headband to pull it back from her face. Studying herself, she tried to identify the look on her face. With astonishment, she realized it was expectation.

One person Shy hoped wouldn't be attending the dance was Renewal's Sheriff. An image of the last time they'd been together still made her blush. The feel of those strong and able hands, caressing, seducing her into madness was too real, too deep a memory to escape without a struggle. She needed distance.

Remembering how quickly she'd responded to his touch, all fire and heat, caused a moan of disbelief to break from her lips.

I was so needy, so wanting. I would have done whatever Cal asked, she thought, cringing in mortification.

Checking her watch, she took one last look in the mirror.

Walking up to the main house, Silvestra resolved to check her nerves at the door and to try and relax.

All thoughts of calm resolve flew out the window when she walked into the den.

"Shy, darlin' you look wonderful!" Mabel kissed her cheek. "Come say hi to Cal."

He was standing by the fireplace, a glass in his hand.

"We thought it would be nice if you had an escort for the dance," Mabel said. "That way you might not feel too self-conscious about not knowing a lot of folks."

Silvestra couldn't think of a reply. In truth, she couldn't think of anything but how incredibly handsome the man standing in front of her looked.

Cal's broad shoulders and torso were encased in a form-fitting plaid shirt, a thin bolero tie wound into the collar. Tight, snug jeans tapering down long legs from the narrow waist almost seemed indecent, they fit so well. His boots were black with polish, buffed to a high shine.

The hairs at the nape of his neck were still damp as if he'd come directly from a shower. When Cal stepped toward her, Shy detected the aroma of cologne, earthy and smelling of the wild outdoors. A tingling sensation wove through her toes and worked up her legs.

"I hope you don't mind," Cal said through a crooked smile.

It took Shy a moment to answer, the smile distracting her from all rational thought. The nerves that she'd hope to squelch showed themselves again in the fluttering going on in her stomach.

"No, that's fine." She was stunned at how calm her voice sounded.

"Well, we'd better get a move on," Jake said. "Don't want to be late."

"Silvestra can ride with me," Cal said, placing a hand at the small of her back.

"That's a good idea. You know how much Mabel loves these things. We never get home before dawn and I wouldn't want you to have to wait around for us, Shy, when you've had enough."

"Dawn, indeed," Mabel exclaimed. "I'm not usually the one who keeps calling for one last reel, Jacob Peter Adams, and you know it."

After helping Silvestra into the truck, Cal easily slid into the cab. Before starting it, he turned and leaned an arm across the seatback.

"I realize this may be a bit uncomfortable for you, especially since Mabel conspired not to tell you until the last minute she'd asked me to come along. But I hope you can get beyond your feelings and have a good time. Renewal barn dances are famous and everyone usually goes home satisfied."

A sigh escaped her. "Mabel's been so good to me. I promised her I'd go and I know she'd be disappointed if I reneged at the last minute."

Cal nodded and turned to start the engine. They drove a bit in silence.

"Did you ever find out anything about Mr. Cambdon's cows?" Silvestra asked at length.

"Necropsy showed enlarged hearts but found no cause. Rand Denny did some tests and sent some blood work out to the county lab. He hasn't heard anything back yet. Have you...seen anything else in the past few days?"

Silvestra shook her head. "No. I've been busy working, finishing up a new book."

They arrived at the dance a few moments later and joined Mabel and Jake at the barn door entrance.

When Cal's hand automatically flew to the small of her back, Silvestra realized, with some small amusement, she was becoming used to the gesture, puzzlingly possessive, yet comforting at the same time.

"Good crowd," Jake said, tapping his foot to the beat of the four-piece band on the stage. "Let's find some seats."

Many heads turned as the two couples angled along the outside of the dance floor. The Adams' waved and smiled when friends called out to them.

"Here's one," Mabel cried, throwing herself down into a seat. "Jake, I would surely love a glass of lemonade."

"Can't we have a dance first? Work up a little sweat?"

"You'll be sweating all over me enough later when you start those feet to twitching. Get me a lemonade and bring one for Shy, too."

"I'll get Silvestra's," Cal offered.

Alone, Mabel took Shy's hand. "I hope you're not mad at me for asking Cal along."

Silvestra's mouth curved wryly. "I understand why you did, Mabel, and I love you for it."

"Oh, darlin', I'm so glad. I just knew you'd have a better time if you had someone to dance with, someone you knew. And he's a great dancer, knows all the new steps to line dancing and everything."

"Obviously you haven't told him what a horrible dancer I am," Shy replied with a groan and an eye roll. "He'd probably never have come if you had."

"Don't put money on that, dear. You'd lose, big time. Oh. Here's Rand Denny. I'll introduce you."

Silvestra turned to see a man similar in age to herself, smiling and walking towards their table. He greeted Mabel with a kiss and then turned his cobalt-colored eyes to her.

"I heard you were visiting from Nate Bolton," Rand said, clasping her outstretched hand. "You were the one who found his cow."

Silvestra nodded and studied the man before her. His handshake had been firm and warm with fellowship, his study of her face more than a polite show of interest. He was attractive in a boyish way with auburn hair in need of a trim, and a long, lanky body he wrapped around the chair next to hers. A broad and open smile traced his face when he propped his elbows on the table and asked, "Are you enjoying your stay?"

Silvestra told him she was then asked him about his veterinary practice. A few minutes later she spied Cal and Jake returning to the table, drinks in their hands.

"Here you go, ladies," Jake said, placing a glass down in front of his wife. "Rand," he added with a nod towards the younger man.

"Rand was just telling us a very amusing story about a rancher over in Carleton and this most amorous bull," Mabel said.

"Here's your lemonade," Cal said. "Denny."

Rand inclined his head in the same manner the Sheriff had, while Cal took a seat next to Silvestra and laid a proprietary arm across the back of her chair.

Silvestra felt the arm, casually draped there, and couldn't understand why the gesture, probably a habit to him, made her feel so sheltered.

"Any news on the Cambdon cows' blood results?" Cal asked.

"None. It usually takes a few days, though, if they find anything, which I don't think they will."

"So you don't suspect anything untoward happened to them?" Silvestra asked.

Denny shrugged. "Nothing *seemed* wrong, I can tell you that. Enlarged hearts, maybe, but that's natural with age and fat. These were beef cattle, bred to be big for sale. Everything else looked normal on the exam. Why? Did you hear something to the contrary?"

Unconsciously, Silvestra's eyes glanced at Cal and then back to the vet's. "No. Nothing."

"Seems strange three of them dying at the same time," Cal said, studying the man. "You didn't find any cause common to all three?"

Silvestra saw Denny's eyes narrow and fix Cal with a level stare. "No, and it's probably because there *was* nothing. If you have some clue as to why they expired, Sheriff, maybe you ought to share it. I'm sure Ben Cambdon would be interested."

"No clues," Cal said easily. "Just some questions. You'll let me know when those blood results come back, won't you?"

Silvestra sensed the subtle antagonism between the men and wondered at its root.

The band, which had just come back from a brief break, began playing. Denny leaned in toward her but Cal cut off whatever he was about to do or say.

"Want to dance?" Rising, he put his hand out for hers.

To Silvestra it didn't sound like a question, more a command. Especially when he stood waiting for her.

As Cal led her to the dance floor, she noticed the questioning stares and whispers behind hands as they made their way out to the middle, joining the other couples ready for a night's fun.

"I think I should warn you I'm not very good at this," she confessed when he took her in his arms.

The corner of his full mouth twitched upward. "Just follow me. It's easy after you go around a few times."

Shy tried to concentrate on his explanations, the direction his feet were taking, but acknowledged with regret, that she had more difficulty than usual. Being in arms that were as strong as steel traps, but she knew could be as gentle and soft as a feather, made focusing a hard task. When they should have been watching his feet, her eyes were drawn to where their hands were joined. The small hairs peeking out from under the plaid cuff, the length of his fingers, straight and taut against hers, took her breath away.

Cal maneuvered around the floor, keeping time with the music, quietly instructing her what to do with each turn. Soon she found herself enjoying the dance - and more- enraptured by the man holding her.

Shy's head whirled. Touching him, being touched, made her mad with longing. She found herself imagining just what it would feel like to have those long, powerful fingers massaging her naked flesh.

Stop it. This can't be and you know it, so just stop your fantasizing right this instant.

Regret competed with the longing, one emotion proving stronger than the other.

The beat of the music quickened as did the dancer's steps. Silvestra heard herself laugh as Cal swirled her around the floor. In one move, he effortlessly twirled her to the right with a flick of his wrist at her waist. She felt as if her flesh had been seared and branded.

Spinning back into his arms, Silvestra stopped short, her body slamming hard into Cal's chest. Instinctively, her hands came up, bracing, on top of his shirt. She could feel his heart hammering, felt the shifting of his rib cage with each breath. She sensed the pulsing of her own blood when his hands came up to enclose her wrists. Head tilting, she found raven-colored eyes burning and bright with an urgent need equaling her own. Insides quaking, she tried desperately to quell the passion surging within. But gazing into those dark mirrors, the small glimmers shifting within them, burning into hers, Silvestra had no will to silence them.

They stayed this way, rooted, each oblivious to the rest of the crowd surrounding them.

Time didn't move.

Eventually, Cal took a deep breath, his gaze never turning from Silvestra's face. "Not bad. I thought you said you didn't dance well."

Shy shook her head.

"I don't," she said, breathless. "You're a remarkable teacher, Sheriff."

Cal's lips twitched again, a gesture she found herself coming to expect from him. A hidden mirth, rarely shown, but one, Silvestra knew, he felt comfortable displaying to her.

"Want to go another round, or would you prefer to sit this one out?"

The desire to stay exactly where they were weighed heavily. When Shy glanced around and discovered they were the sole occupants of the dance floor, a deep flush flew up her cheeks.

"I think I'd like to have that lemonade now," she said.

He nodded and silently led her back to the table, empty now, as Jake and Mabel made the rounds of their friends.

No sooner had Silvestra drained her glass, than a purring noise sounded from behind her.

"Look Ben, honey, it's Cal. Let's say hello."

Shy turned and found Priscilla Bolton coming towards them, Ben Cambdon's arm draped casually around her shoulders. The tube top dress she wore flared out at the waist and ended just above the knees, showing the young woman's slender legs off to full advantage. The snug-fitting bodice outlined the swell of full breasts bouncing seductively as she walked. Copper curls were gathered high on her head, little wisps provocatively slipping loose.

Priscilla Bolton looked and smelled like sex, raw and primal. Shy knew every male in the room recognized it.

"Nice to see you again, Silvestra," Ben said, pulling a chair for Priscilla and then seating himself between the women.

"Ben," Silvestra smiled. "Priscilla."

The younger woman smiled in return, but Shy could see the greeting held no warmth. When the holly-colored eyes turned to Cal, she read the blazon desire nestled in them.

"Haven't seen you lately, Cal, honey. Been busy lockin' up the poor rabble?"

Her voice sounds like natural honey flowing from a hive and I wouldn't want to be the person she sets her stinger for, Silvestra thought.

"Now and again," Cal replied, easily, slinking his hand behind Shy's chair. Priscilla bristled at the gesture.

Coyly slanting her eyes, Pris laid one well-manicured hand across her date's and said, "Ben was just telling me about the trouble he had with those cows dying. Strange thing, that. Are you investigating it?"

"Looking into it."

"Strange," she repeated, rubbing her fingers over Ben's knuckles. "Ben told me you knew about the cows even before he did. How'd you manage that? Some old-fashioned mysticism?"

It was Silvestra's turn to bristle. Her spine snapped to attention.

"Now, Pris," Ben interrupted, laying one of his hands over hers. "This is an evening to have some fun, not to talk about bad situations. Cal is doing his job, just as Rand Denny is. I'm sure my animals died from nothing more than old age, that's all. Are you enjoying the dance Silvestra," he asked, turning to her with a smile across his face.

Biting back the retort she badly wanted to make, Shy took a deep breath and said, "Yes, I am. Immensely."

"This is her first square dance," Cal said, rubbing her shoulder with the heel of his thumb.

"Really? Well, we'll have to make it a memorable one," Ben said.

"I'm surprised," Priscilla said, idly inspecting one of her fingernails. "I'd think this was all pretty borin' and tame for you, being from the East and all."

"Excuse me?" Shy said.

Priscilla's smile was rancorous, baring lots of teeth and lips. "Well, I just mean you're probably used to ballroom dancing, champagne cocktails, and such. This must seem pretty hokey to someone as sophisticated as you. I can see you being guided around the dance floor in the arms of a man in whitetails, not blue jeans. Square dancing can get pretty lively, you know. It's very different from waltzing."

"Is that so?" Shy said easily, recognizing the bait the younger woman was tossing. "Well, I may not be an expert at such lively dancing, but in fact," she said, turning to Cal and bestowing a wildly flirtatious grin on him, "I'm finding it more fun than I imagined. Caleb is a marvelous dancer. I feel like I can dance anything when I'm with him."

Shy was rewarded by seeing fury leap into the green eyes facing her.

"Yes, as a matter of fact, I do," Pris said, tossing her head.

Silvestra read the jealousy written across Pris's pretty face and knew the younger woman was trying to figure out another way to annoy and rankle her.

Before she could, Ben said, "Well, I'm not too bad myself. Care to have a whirl with me?"

Shy's smile was as wide as Priscilla's frown was tight.

"I'd love to," she said taking his hand and throwing Cal a conspiratorial smile.

The Sheriff watched the duo head for the dance floor and thought - not for the first time - that Silvestra Coeltrain was *some* woman. She'd put Pris in her very well deserved place and had managed to do it looking like a true queen.

He sensed Shy had been riled by Priscilla's nasty remarks, and he'd willingly allowed himself to be used to aggravate the woman in return. His reward had been the coy, coquettish smile Shy gave him for Priscilla's benefit. Unbeknownst to Silvestra, though, that smile had delighted him.

"I don't ever remember you smiling at me like that," Pris said, interrupting his thoughts.

"What way?"

"Like a man who knows a woman in the most intimate of ways. You seem to be getting very friendly with the New York Lady."

At the unmistakable edge of pettiness in her voice, Cal refused to be lured into responding in kind. "Boston."

"Boston, what?"

"She's from Boston, not New York."

Priscilla clucked her tongue and waved her hand carelessly. "Whatever."

Cal's black brows rose fractionally as he saw Silvestra laugh at something Ben said. Head tossed back, eyes crinkled at the corners with mirth, he watched as she danced in the arms of a man he considered a friend, and was astounded at the small stab of jealousy slicing through him. Banking the feeling, he refused to give in to its weakness and toyed with the idea of how to make Silvestra smile at him as she had before. The possibilities were promising.

Priscilla, in a bold and obvious move, switched chairs, placing herself next to Cal in the seat Silvestra had vacated. Cal watched out of the corner of his eye as she moved her chair closer to his. When a freshly manicured hand slunk under the table to massage his thigh, Cal kept his eyes and voice level, shifting one leg over the other, away from her touch

"I've missed you, Cal, honey," she whispered into his ear, oblivious to the stares of those seated at tables around them. Nipping his earlobe, she added, "Missed you in my life, in my bed. Why don't we just go now? No one will miss us. I only came with Ben because I knew you'd be here. I know you want me, you always have. We're good together, good for each other." Her hand found the buckle on his belt and wormed one finger beneath it, pressing against the flesh of his stomach.

Cal's muscles contracted, but not from need. "Priscilla," he said, evenly, trying to curtail the disgust rising up within him. "Stop it. Now,"

Ignoring him, she leaned closer, blowing out a small breath on his cheek, nuzzling it with her nose. "You can't have forgotten the last time we were together, what I did for you," she said, lowering her voice. "I know everything it takes to make you happy, Cal. Everything. I'll bet my last dollar little Miss Boston doesn't know what it takes to satisfy a man like you. I'll wager she never could be what I've been to you."

A strangled oath exploded between his teeth as he shoved his chair back and stood. Looking down at her, his repulsion plainly written in his eyes and the scowl across his mouth, he said tightly, "You're right about that, Pris. Silvestra only knows how to be a lady, not a whore."

He turned and stalked towards the dance floor.

Green eyes, filled with hatred, followed him.

Chapter Six

A few minutes later, Cal managed to curb his anger. Once he was holding Silvestra, once she was in his arms, leaning toward him as the band played a ballad, one hand delicately cupped into his, Cal exhaled deeply.

"I've always loved this song," Silvestra told him. "It's so sad."

Charmed by her, the chuckle bubbled up from deep within his chest. "Most love songs *are* sad," he said, staring down at her face.

Her lips curled into a grin.

"I'm sorry about Priscilla," he said before he could stop himself. "She had no right to speak to you so rudely."

"Don't worry about it," she said, shrugging her delicate shoulders. "She sees me as a threat, I guess, and just wants to protect what's hers. I've been treated worse in my life and by people with more power and more class than Priscilla Bolton."

Two phrases stuck in his mind. "Silvestra, not now nor have I ever belonged to Pris. We shared a few laughs, and for a time we were lovers. But we never belonged together."

Not like you and I do, he wanted to add.

She looked up into his face and nodded.

"How have you been treated worse?" he asked.

The shake of her head was careless, but the hurt that skirted by in her eyes was stark. "People who didn't believe my visions were real. Detectives, mostly who assumed what I saw were the imaginative ravings of a woman seeking fame through publicity. A woman who would use grieving families to make a name for herself. That's a direct quote, by the way."

Cal cradled her closer, wanting to comfort, wanting to defend. "Has it always been so hard to get people to believe you?"

Shy was quiet a moment, swaying her body to the beguiling beat of the music.

"Officials, yes. Parents or other loved ones are usually more receptive. They'll try anything they can to get their child back. Especially if I can connect to the one missing, see where they are, or get a feeling for what's happening to them. The first time I helped the police -"

Cal watched her eyes flutter. Lowering her head, she said, "I'm sorry. I don't usually blabber on like that."

"Go on. I'd like to hear about it."

The tempo slowed even more as the band began another sultry ballad. Cal never heard the change in the cadence. The dozens of couples surrounding them, hanging on to one another while the music played, were invisible to him. All he could see, hear, all he wanted, was the woman he held in his arms.

"I was sixteen," she said. "Still in high school. Boarding school, actually. I was sitting in art class one day when my hands went numb and I saw the face of a little girl cross through my mind. I can remember exactly what she looked like. Six or seven, just beginning a growth spurt, her arms were longer than her legs. Long, red hair braided over each ear. She was missing the two incisors on top and one tooth on the bottom. Her skin was very fair and I could see the bluish tint of veins beneath its whiteness. The image was so stark, for a second I thought she must have walked past me. Then it was gone. After class, I went back to the dorm and my roommate had the television on. The little girl's face was a still photograph on one part of the screen, a written physical description, and a phone number to call underneath in another. Her name was Kiera Dralaney and she'd been missing from home for two days."

Cal's eyes never left her face as she told the story. Her voice, soft as a zephyr, glided over him.

"What did you do?"

She let out a soul-weary sigh and laid her head against the vast expanse of his chest, nestling into it as if born to rest there.

"The first thing I did was sit down and try to catch my breath. I was scared because I could feel the girl's terror washing through me. I knew she'd been taken by someone close to her."

"How?"

She shook her head. "It's unexplainable. I could sense she'd trusted this person and then grew frightened. I wanted to call the police but was afraid they'd think I was crazy. Instead, I laid down to take a nap. I was exhausted. That's when I had the second flash and knew where she was."

"Tell me," Cal whispered into her hair.

"It was a small room, six by six feet square. On one wall a television was tuned to the local news. She was watching a story about her own disappearance, one ankle shackled to the wall. She was screaming at the television telling it where she was, begging to be saved."

"*Jesus.*" Cal's grip tightened around her body.

"I knew I had to go to the police then." She took a deep breath, then let it out slowly. "They grilled me for six hours, even called my parents and my shrink to confirm I wasn't crazy, wasn't having delusions or ideations. They wrote down every piece of descriptive information I could give about the room, every single detail. I told them it was in a private home, in a cool place, where no noise could get to it, in a home close to Kiera's."

"What made them believe you?"

"That's the funny part. They didn't give out every detail on the news about the disappearance. They'd kept back one vital piece of information."

Cal nodded, knowing it as a common police tactic. Don't reveal everything, then when you get someone in with information, make them tell you what's missing.

"It's a way of weeding out the nut cases, the publicity seekers," he said.

"I know. They thought that's what I was. But I knew the piece of the puzzle they held quietly in their hands."

"What was it?"

"Kiera had a stuffed rabbit she always kept close. Slept with her, went to school with her."

"And it wasn't still in the house?"

"Yes, it was. That told the police she went willingly with the person because she knew she wasn't going far."

"Substantiating what you'd said about the abductor being someone she trusted."

"Exactly. Once I told them, they started believing me."

"What did the cops do with all the information you provided?"

"Called the girl's parents in and told them. The father ran from the room before the Chief Detective finished. He flew from the station, jumped into his car, and sped away, ten uniformed police following behind. He knew, you see, where that room was."

Shy lifted her gaze to Cal's.

"Mr. Dralaney drove to a house three blocks from his. He busted down the front door and was beating the owner almost to death before the police arrived and stopped him. He told them where the room was, how to get to it. It was located in a subbasement under a shed in the backyard."

"In a cool place," Cal murmured, pulling her back, letting her head fall on his chest again.

She nodded. "Behind a false wall; the room was soundproof, encased in lead."

"No noise. The little girl? Was she -?"

"They found her awake and crying. Her father rushed her to the hospital himself, the police escorting them. Physically she was fine. Mentally," Shy shrugged, "well, who'll ever know for sure just exactly what damage a trauma like that can cause?"

"The person who took her?" Cal found he was almost afraid to know the answer.

Shy pulled back and stared up at him, her gaze unwavering. "Her uncle. The mother's brother."

An oath similar in scope and emotion to the one he'd used earlier with Priscilla, broke from him. "What happened to you after that?"

"The local newspaper got hold of the story from the girl's parents. They thought what I'd done was so wonderful they wanted the world to know about it." Shy laughed, a bitter and harsh sound Cal found disturbing. "After that, a national news wire picked up the story and for months I was inundated with phone calls and letters from people begging me, pleading, offering me ridiculous sums of money, to find their missing loved ones. I couldn't help them all, of course. Some had good results, some...well, not so good. Tragic. I couldn't help them all," She repeated.

Cal recognized the desperation in her voice as guilt.

The cloud that started in her eyes drifted down to the rest of her face. "I lost twenty pounds and wound up in the hospital, treated for exhaustion and malnutrition."

Knowing what he now did about her, Cal gave voice to a question that had been plaguing him for days. "Did you have a vision the day I found you fishing?"

Amber eyes bore into his.

"Yes."

"I thought so. When I felt your hands they were ice cold just like you explained. What did you see?"

She shook her head and cast her gaze downward. "It was...personal. I really don't want to get into it."

He accepted it, nodded, and glanced around the dance floor. They were the only couple still pressed together, dancing to a love song. All the other dancers had separated into a lively two-step.

"Come on," he said, grabbing her hand. He pushed through the throng of people milling about, through the barn entrance until they were outside, never leaving go of Silvestra's hand.

The night air had cooled, bringing with it a refreshing crispness. Crickets sang loudly close by, natural competition for the band.

Cal led her around the outer perimeter of the barn, towards the back parking lot. Once he was certain they were away from prying eyes and ears, he stopped.

Turning to Silvestra, he saw the golden glow of the moon reflected over her head and wondered, for just a second, if she could possibly be real.

"You're beautiful in the moonlight, Silvestra. But then, I've found you're beautiful at any time."

His hands found their way to her upper arms, gently pulling her towards him. "I've been dreaming about doing this since the last time we were together."

Her eyes widened just a fraction when he brought his head down. Her face lifted to his, a look of open anticipation dancing across it.

With a swiftness born of desperation and cutting need, Cal's mouth claimed hers.

When her lips parted on a sigh, he needed no further invitation. A swift swipe of his tongue and he was inside her mouth, probing, exploring. She tasted sweet and full of spice, and so very alive. His heart pounded against his chest, nearly exploding with excitement. The two brief kisses they'd shared were mild temptations, when, once taken, could no longer be ignored. Silvestra's mouth moved under his and Cal groaned with need. One hand cupped the nape of her neck as he bent her back across his arm, deepening the kiss. The gasp he heard escape from her thrilled him, spurred him on.

His other hand slinked down her neck, past her shoulders, to rest in the hollow below her breast. Resting his palm against the gentle swell, his thumb flicked across the center. He was rewarded with the nipple hardening instantly beneath the fabric of her dress.

Silvestra arched against him, molding to his form as small mews of pleasure rose from her throat.

Cal's mouth began a slow descent from her lips, down her neck. When he nipped at the fleshy part of her earlobe, he smiled in delight as she fisted her fingers into his hair, yanking his head further in its exploration.

Silvestra wanted him, of that he was certain. Her body wouldn't react this way if she didn't. But would she respond to that wanting? Or would she be shattered with guilt, tormented by her need? A husband, waiting at home. A son, too.

Cal tried to banish the thoughts. For the moment, for this one special moment, she was his, not another's.

A wonderful warmth stretched within him; a sensation of rightness followed it.

Silvestra's mind stopped the moment Cal's tongue parted her lips. A thousand shards of light ripped through her flesh at the intimacy of his touch. Fingers, toes, mouth, all tingled with desire. Heat spread throughout her body, igniting and heightening every nerve fiber, making each caress an eruption of pleasure.

A creamy glow expanded through her. He had the power to stir her as she'd never been stirred before. Emotions swirling and jumping mingled within her.

All Silvestra wanted, all she could see, hear, touch...was Cal.

Her hands slaked up his torso, marveling at the masculine feel of him. He was solid, hard; the most physically intense man she'd ever known. Every move he made screamed *male.* Yet his hands, so strong, glided over her with the softest of caresses.

Silvestra's hands flew up to his hair, met and twined, astounded at the luxurious feel and texture of it. Jet-black hair that looked like coal, felt like silk.

Something roused from deep within her, begging to be released. For one brief moment, Silvestra thought she recognized it.

Cal pulled back from the kiss and sighed. "Silvestra," he whispered into her hair, cradling her close.

"How do you do that?" she asked, gazing openly at him.

Cal ran a finger down the line of her cheek, resting it on her bottom lip, now swollen from his kisses. "What?"

"Make me want you so much just by saying my name?"

Cal's finger stopped moving.

"No man's ever done that to me before."

There was wonder in her voice, awe of the truth she'd spoken.

With infinite care and tenderness, Cal lowered his lips to hers again, barely touching them.

It was a kiss that told Silvestra everything he felt, every emotion running through him, every care he intended to take.

This was a man who could make her feel again; make her want again; make her whole again. On a sigh, she closed her eyes and let the knowledge freely soak through her.

With it came the expected doubt.

But can I? Can I feel again? Will I ever be whole?

The prick of fear that stabbed at her heart wouldn't abate.

"Silvestra, open your eyes and look at me."

She did.

"I want you more, in this instant, than any woman I've ever wanted before." Laying his chin on the top of her head, Cal sighed again. "What are we going to do about this?"

It was a question that had been swimming around in her head, drowning but for an answer since he'd pulled her from the dance floor. Head securely nestled against his chest, she could hear his heart pounding, drumming, beating with longing.

I want him so desperately. It's as if my life depends on it.

Examining the surprising emotion, Silvestra thought it was simple lust, primal and needy. She'd been without a man for so long. A deeply sensual and feeling woman, she tried to explain her emotions away rationally.

But somewhere, down in the recesses of her soul, Silvestra knew she was wrong.

Her sigh matched his. "I wish I knew."

"We could use some of that psychic mysticism Pris referred to about now."

Because his words echoed the thought that had drifted through her, Silvestra laughed.

Cal pulled back just enough to view her face. "You don't read crystal balls, do you?" he asked, one eyebrow cocked to his hairline, mouth trying to stay in a straight line.

Silvestra shook her head. "Don't read tarot cards or palms, either."

"I was afraid of that."

His face was so serious, so devoid of all the good-natured joking his words implied, she burst out laughing again.

"I love the way you laugh," Cal said, tracing her lips with his own. "It's a sound I could hear forever and never tire of."

The words touched her in a silent place long thought dead. Staring up at his face, eyes so black she could barely see them in the darkness, Silvestra's heart stopped.

No, this wasn't lust, wasn't fundamental need. Lust would wither and fade when the passion was spent. This was more; much more.

Was it possible to fall so completely in love in such a short time?

For, it was love. Total and consuming.

How had this happened? How could it?

Her heart had dried and withered long ago when everything that meant anything had been destroyed. The life she'd known had been ripped apart, torn away, and with it, Silvestra thought, her capacity to love.

How is it possible to love this man, she asked herself again. From the edge of her mind came the answer. This was a man who made her feel alive, made her feel wanted, treasured. A man who could ignite her blood with a look, make her head spin with a touch. This was a man whose past, battles, and demons had made him the person he was today. They were soul mates in that, Silvestra thought. The heart she'd thought dead and buried was resurrected by the emotions Caleb Blackbear churned within her. Emotions she'd never expected to surface again

I love him.

The thought thrilled and terrified her.

"I can't and won't deny I want you, Silvestra," Cal said, breaking the silence. "I have since the first time I saw you. You can't deny you feel it too, this attraction, this connection we have to one another."

"No, I won't deny it," she answered in a soft, yet firm voice. "I do want you, but -"

"No. No 'buts'." He laid a finger across her lips and then replaced it with his mouth. "No buts now," he repeated. "I know this is hard for you. You have... obligations...responsibilities. I know you're confused, maybe as much as I am. I've never been the kind of man who takes after another man's woman," he said, with a crooked smile.

Silvestra's eyebrows shot up. "Another man's -"

"Shush, darlin'. The fact that you're here and he's a thousand miles away tells me a few things. We don't have to go into them." Cal paused, and pulled Silvestra closer in his arms, tracing his hands up and down her back, in her hair. She could feel his heart beating against her chest. "I only care about being with you, Silvestra, getting to know you, everything about you. I just want to be with you. It's almost like we were meant to meet, to be with one another. I can't explain it, don't have the words. I only know what I feel for you is something I've never felt before. I don't want to lose it."

Maybe it was because he said it so humbly, so honestly. Silvestra would try and convince herself later that was the reason she'd kept silent about Paul. Telling him now would only confuse matters more.

She wanted Cal; she loved him. And he wanted her. For too long she'd shut herself away, cocooned in a private world, isolated from people, from feelings, from any chance of love. With Cal she was becoming reborn; renewed. He knew next to nothing about her, about her past, and yet he wanted to be with her, simply be with her.

How can I tell him about Paul? I know I should. I will. Soon, but not now. This is too fresh, too new.

Soon, she promised herself. I'll tell him soon.

For now, she'd just accept being with him. It was easier, less complicated to let Cal think she belonged to someone else. It would protect both of them for a while longer.

But I *will* tell him the truth.

Taking his hand, she kissed the knuckles, heard the swift hiss of his breath hitching, and said, "All right. No buts. For now."

He smiled back, broadly. "Well, then, how about a few more dances? My feet are about ready to be trod on again."

"Oh."

Her eyes widened, then slanted, a response that set laughter bursting from him.

"I thought I was doing so well, too," she said, pouting.

When she tried to flounce away, a quick yank pulled her back. The air pushed from the bottom of her lungs, up and out in one felled swoop when they banged together.

For a few magical moments, where the world was a distant universe and all the complications of their lives were nullified, they stood, locked in one another's embrace.

Cal's mouth came to hers slowly, torpidly. When their lips met, a fire burst between them, the flames of their passion building at a rapid pace. Emotions, fresh and primitive spun above and around them, dazzling them both.

Silvestra was the first to break the spell. Drawing back, her breathing barely under control, she licked her lips, reveling in his taste, and said, "I promise I'll try not to wreak havoc on your toes again."

Cal's mouth curled at the corners. "Well, my boots are pretty thick. They can take just about anything."

Smiling, he wound her arm in his and led them both back to the barn.

Chapter Seven

It was a magnificent morning.

The air was warm and dry with a suggestion of a breeze billowing about. The sun stood high and bright, the sky a cloudless azure. Silvestra could see for miles in front of her. The land was exquisite, untamed, untouched. She could imagine it thousands of years ago. Except for the reality of the present looming up ahead, it might have looked just this way.

Silvestra's smile grew as she remembered the evening before. The dance had been fun - more than that. It had been like a coming out party. She'd forgotten what it was like to enjoy herself, to be with people, with one person you cared for. To laugh, and kiss under the moonlight. Silvestra experienced all that with Cal.

When he'd brought her home well past 2 a.m., he'd smothered her with a lingering kiss at the door, making her mind blank to everything around them. Even Solomon's persistent barking went unnoticed. His kisses were consuming, devouring, and totally wonderful.

She could have stayed in his arms all night. The comfort and solace she found there were a natural remedy for the dark malady she'd faced the past year. Just when she'd thought to invite him in, Cal pulled away, saying he'd better go.

Silvestra watched him fight an internal battle when he started to leave. She knew he wanted to stay, but realized he would only if she asked him to.

What she felt for him was too raw, too confusing. She needed time to get used to the idea of loving a man again. To give herself physically was a fear she needed to overcome.

Somehow, she felt Cal instinctively knew this, for, with one last blistering kiss, he'd tipped his hat and closed the door behind him.

Now, Silvestra leaned Mabel's old bike up against the brick wall and went in. The office looked a great deal like she'd imagined it would. Square, with a wood floor and a high ceiling. Three desks, arranged in a triangular fashion around the perimeter of the room, a computer terminal, and a screen at one. The walls were an antiseptic white, the furniture dark brown. A book stand filled almost to bursting with books occupied one wall; a coffee maker, fax machine, and printer sat on a table at another.

An ordinary office.

But the man seated across from the door, who now rose to greet her, was anything but ordinary. He filled the room, dwarfing it, as he came toward her, a candid smile on his lips.

Silvestra's cheeks grew hot under his gaze, her stomach warm with desire. Breathing already rapid from the bike ride accelerated when his eyes traversed her face. She recognized the look he wore. She'd seen it in the mirror that very morning when she found herself thinking about him.

Hunger. Pure and simple hunger, the likes of which would never be sated with mere food.

At that moment, she knew what it would be like to be devoured whole.

"Silvestra," he said, taking her hand.

They stood, holding hands, staring at one another for an eternity.

"I brought these for Summer and Winter," she said, finding her voice.

Cal looked towards the small bundle she cradled in her arms.

"I had my publisher Fed Ex them. They're all inscribed and signed."

"Your books."

"What was it they said? All their friends would die of pea-green envy?"

Cal's lips twitched at the corners. "Something like that."

Taking them and carrying them like some sort of precious and fragile glassware, he laid them on the desk. "They're going to be thrilled," he said. Holding both her hands now, Cal pulled Silvestra to him, nuzzling her cheek with his nose. "I bet folks in the next county will hear those two whooping and screaming with delight. It was very sweet of you."

Silvestra never got the chance to reply. Suddenly, Cal's mouth found hers and pushed all rational thought and speech from her mind.

Without a notion not to, she surrendered to the kiss, to the embrace, to everything he had to give her.

"*Harumph.*"

At the sound, she jumped back, eyes wide with surprise. She hadn't seen Deputy Dickensen, didn't know he was in the office as well, since all she could see was Cal. Heat ran up her neck and cheeks.

Placing nervous hands in the pockets of her jeans, Silvestra cleared her throat and sent Harv a shy, embarrassed smile. "Good morning, Deputy."

"Ma'am."

Cal leaned a hip against one of the desks and folded his arms across his chest. "Did you ride into town?"

"Yes. Mable's bike's outside."

"Well then, you've probably worked up an appetite. How about an early lunch over at Reva's? She makes the best chicken and gravy around."

Embarrassment flown, Shy gave him a lopsided smile. "It can't be as good as Mabel's.

"Come and judge for yourself."

The mischievous light in his eyes, so in contrast to the natural blackness, stirred her.

"Okay. You're on."

Cal tossed a quick glance at Harv. "I'll be at Reva's if you need me." He slid his hat from the rack, put it in place, and took Shy's arm. Folding it into the crook of his elbow, he added, "But try not to need me."

The second the office was empty, Harv picked up the phone and dialed. "Sherry, you're never gonna believe this in a million years."

"So what do you think? Better than Mabel's?"

Shy leaned back, still chewing. After swallowing, she said, "Different, but I don't know if it's better. It's delicious, though."

"You're just being loyal. A trait, by the way, I find admirable."

Her laugh, so free and easy, kicked him right in the stomach.

The shadows he'd seen under her eyes a few days ago had all but disappeared.

He watched her eat, taking pleasure in seeing how hungry she'd been. The plate of chicken, gravy, biscuits, and mashed potatoes Reva herself piled high, was almost empty.

"You did work up an appetite riding in." He grinned.

Shy groaned and leaned back in the booth. "If I keep this up I'll go home weighing three hundred pounds. It's bad enough Mabel feeds me as if I were three people."

Home.

The word sat heavily on his chest.

For a brief time, Cal had let himself believe she wouldn't be going anywhere, that she'd stay in Renewal, stay, hopefully, with him. The fantasy he'd played out in his mind of the two of them together was one Cal had hoped to turn into reality. Shy's casual mention of going home made him face the truth of the situation.

Home.

To a husband, a son, and a lifestyle he had no part in. The sudden, quick stab of pain slicing through him shook Cal's very soul.

When did I fall in love with her? Why did she claim my heart when she belongs to someone else?

The question sparked an angry surge within him. But along with it came a determination he found familiar. All his life Cal had been fighting. First for acceptance in a white man's world, a world not kind to anyone it considered different. He'd been beaten and tormented all through school for not being an anglo. In college, where he thought maturity would bring acceptance, he found only contempt. His toughest battle had been deciding to return home to a town that had scorned his parents for marrying and to fight for a job he knew he could do better than any other man in Renewal. Cal found the struggle well worth the effort. He loved this town, his job, and the woman seated across from him, a mouthful of biscuit with melting butter dripping down her flawless chin.

Cal thought his fighting days were behind him but realized they'd only just begun.

Shy let out a surprised yelp when his hand reached over and flicked the dripping butter from her jaw. When he brought his finger to his mouth, licking it clean of the oily taste, her pupils dilated.

"There you are. Stuffing your face as usual. I swear, all you do is work and eat."

Plopping down next to Cal, she said, "Harv told me you were here having lunch." Turning to Silvestra, she added, "Hi. I'm Rose, Cal's sister."

Shy extended her hand. "Silvestra Coeltrain."

"Oh, I *know* who you are," Rose said, tapping a finger to Shy's forearm. "My daughters have been ridiculously giddy these past few days since they met you. Living with thirteen-year-old twins is hard enough. Living with them when they've been bowled over is exhausting."

Shy's laugh came freely.

"Silvestra just dropped off a package of her books for the girls. They're autographed and inscribed," Cal said.

Rose dropped her head into her hands. "There'll be no living with them now. I'll need to move."

Cal glanced at Shy and smiled.

"Seriously," Rose said a heartbeat later. "They'll be thrilled. On their behalf I thank you."

"I hope they enjoy them. Your daughters are very sweet."

"Oh, they're sweet all right, especially when they want something. Which, by the way, is why I'm here." Rose turned to her brother and asked, "Are you free Saturday night?"

Cal cast a swift glance at Silvestra. "That depends," he said, breaking off a piece of biscuit and handing it to his sister. "What's up?"

"The girls want to go to the movies in Marlough. Something silly about a teenage girl in L.A. and how she insinuates herself into the lives of her friends. I can't drive them because I've got a teacher's conference and Kenny's in Jackson for the weekend at a grain conference. Can you take them?"

"Depends," he repeated, turning back to Silvestra. "You feel like coming along? I could use some help with those two. They can be real monsters when they want to be. Having you along may keep'em calm."

"Great, Cal, give her a big buildup until she can't wait to go," Rose said, rolling her eyes. "And didn't Mama teach you a better way to ask a lady out than that?"

Cal's heart skipped a few beats when he saw Silvestra blush. He'd purposefully made his invitation lighthearted, hoping to allay any fears she might have of going out with him. Using the twins as an excuse was, in his mind, the perfect ruse.

"Silvestra, I heartily apologize for my brother's ridiculously boorish request."

The blush disappeared. "I think it sounds like fun," she said after a moment. "I can't remember the last time I saw a movie, and I'm sure I'll have a great time with the girls."

Cal let out the breath he hadn't realized he was holding.

"Great," Rose said, patting Shy's hand. "Thank you. The girls are simply going to explode. Their favorite uncle and their favorite author. I don't know if I'll be able to live with them until the weekend."

"I'm their only uncle, by the way." He turned his attention to Silvestra and the smile was abruptly wiped away. "What's wrong?"

She'd gone white. Snowcap white. Her eyes had turned to glass and she'd dropped the fork onto the plate as if it weighed more than she could manage.

"Silvestra?" He reached for her hand. The icy cold feel of it shocked him. When he looked down at her hands, saw how mottled they'd become, he knew instantly what was happening.

Rose stared at the woman across from her, shocked by the sudden change. "Cal--?"

"She's seeing something," he explained, his eyes never leaving Shy's face. "She's psychic."

Rose's black eyes widened, then relaxed. "Like grandma?"

Cal shook his head. "More. Different."

Silvestra's skin turned to chalk and Cal silently cursed, grabbing both of her hands. He wanted urgently to warm her. He knew he had to let her be, let the vision run its course.

Silvestra stared ahead, sitting ramrod straight. The pulsing at her temple was worrisome and he wanted to kiss it smooth again. Gently stroking a finger down to her wrist he was astounded at the unusually slow heart rate. A quick glance at her chest confirmed her breathing had also slowed.

At this rate, she'll pass out.

"How long does this last?" Rose asked.

Cal heard the sympathy in her voice and was touched by it. "I don't know. I think each one is unique, time-wise."

They both continued staring at her. Suddenly, her fingers began to warm beneath his touch. Cal stared into her eyes and saw some life coming back into them. Her color was still pale, but the breathing had picked up pace once again.

"She's coming out of it," Rose said.

Shy blinked a few times, shook her head from side to side. When her vision cleared, she stared across the table and whispered, "Cal."

He recognized the raw edge to her voice: fear. Squeezing her hands, he said, "You saw something."

She nodded, tears welling up in her eyes. Cal's grip tightened.

"Ten of them...together...lying together in a row...oh, God." She yanked back her hands and dropped her head into them.

"Cattle?"

Shy nodded. Raising her head, she looked at him, the tears falling freely down her cheeks. "All dead."

Cal's lips tightened. "Can you tell me where?"

She started to describe the place she'd seen when Harv burst through the doors of Reva's, his eyes wide and searching. When they fixed on Cal, he quickly made his way to their booth.

"Sorry to interrupt, Cal, but I just got a call from Amos Pierce over at the Lazy Q. Seems they found ten dead head of cattle in the back pasture."

"This is exactly what I saw," Silvestra said.

It had taken them almost twenty minutes to drive out to the Lazy Q. In the squad, all three had been silent.

They were met at the ranch by one of the field cowboys and escorted to the pasture where the cows had been discovered.

Alighting from the car, the smell hit them like a slap in the face.

"Jumpin' Jiminy!" Harv's hand flew to cover his nose and mouth.

"This is what I saw," Silvestra repeated.

Harv's head snapped around to her. "Ma'am?"

"Never mind," Cal said, the terse edge in his voice a warning.

Cal walked to the group of men surrounding the animals, Shy and Harv following.

"Amos," Cal greeted the owner with a nod. "Denny."

The vet, squatting next to one of the animals, oblivious to the flies swirling around its lifeless mouth, said, "Sheriff," curtly, never removing his eyes from his work. He examined the cow's mouth as he pulled back the fatty lips, tugged on the swollen tongue.

"What happened, Amos?" Cal asked.

"Damned if I know. Sam, he found'em, laid out like matchbox cars, stiff as boards."

The Sheriff turned to the man he knew to be the foreman.

Sam Rockwell's weathered hands shook violently and Cal was quick to notice the greenish cast to the older man's skin.

"Sam?"

"I- I noticed we was missing a few this morning, Sheriff, when me and the boys brought the herd out to graze." He licked his parched lips and swallowed hard. "Dick and me went off to try and find the strays. I came around the bend and saw that one over there, with its legs up. Closer I got, the smell told me it was dead. Then I saw the rest. Honest to

God, Sheriff, I ain't never seen so many dead at once like that. Just laid down and died, sweet as you please. It don't make no sense."

Cal nodded, pushing his hat back from his forehead. "No, it doesn't." He saw Silvestra approach one of the cattle as his eyes found Rand.

"Anything Denny?"

"I've only been here a minute more than you. Give me a chance to do my work."

"*Sheriff.*"

Cal turned towards the urgent plea and found Silvestra in the arms of one of the cowboys. Her color had turned to paste.

"She passed clear out," the cowboy said as Cal shot over to them like lightning. "Touched that cow there, I watched her do it, then kind of moaned and I could see she was gonna go down. Caught her before she did."

"Lay her down," Cal ordered. The hitch in his voice was sharp. Maneuvering between them, Cal took Shy's head into his lap and softly called her name. When her eyelids fluttered, he felt his heart start beating again.

"Cal," she said, tears instantly flowing down her cheeks.

"Shush, it's all right."

"No, no it isn't," Shy said, attempting to lean forward to a sitting position. "These animals didn't die naturally."

Squinting down at her he said, "What?"

"They were killed. Purposely and methodically killed."

Chapter Eight

It took almost two hours before he could get Silvestra home.

After hearing her shocking statement, Amos Pierce went wild.

"What in hell is she talking about? Who would want to kill my cattle? Who would dare?"

Cal tried to calm the man, but his tirade would not be checked.

"And how does she know they've been killed?" He pointed to Silvestra. "What's going on here, Sheriff? Dammit, I want to know. Those cows were scheduled for auction next week and I'd say I just lost me almost two hundred thousand in sales. I want to know what the hell this woman knows."

It was Silvestra who finally managed to quell Pierce's verbal storm. She stood, shakily at best, squared her shoulders, and told the rancher who she was and what she was able to do. The shocked stares and disbelieving snickers of the men surrounding them put murder in Cal's eyes. Dedication to his badge held him back.

Amos quieted after that, for which Cal was grateful.

Placing Silvestra in the squad, dismayed to see her still shaking, Cal and Harv began interviewing the cowboys.

No one had seen anything out of the ordinary in the last day at the ranch; no visitors; nothing amiss with the herd.

"They've been dead between twelve to eighteen hours," Denny said.

"Notice any similarities between these and Ben Cambdon's?" Cal asked.

The vet replaced his instruments in his medical bag and shot a quizzical look at the Sheriff. "You think they're related?"

Cal shrugged. "Don't know, but it seems like we should examine a connection between them. Two different herds, each with multiple and simultaneous deaths. Makes me wonder."

"Your lady friend think they're related?"

"She hasn't mentioned it, but it's strange both herds have been affected the same way. You find anything, and I mean *anything* similar between them when you slice them up, you be sure to let me know immediately. Understand?"

Denny nodded.

Settled in the squad, Cal told Harv he would drop him back at the office and then take Silvestra home.

Reticently, Harv turned to Shy. "Is it true, ma'am, that you can, well, you know? Do that? See things that are gonna happen, in your mind. Like that Jean Dixon?"

Cal glanced in the rearview mirror. Shy's smile was a tired one and her eyes had grown heavy.

"I can't predict earthquakes or rain, Deputy, but yes, I can feel things sometimes."

"Silvestra usually works with law enforcement agencies on missing person cases," Cal said.

"No kidding?" Harv's eyes widened.

Shy's smile was her reply, sleepy though it was. In the rearview mirror, Cal saw her yawn, cover her mouth and then fight to keep her eyes open.

He floored the gas.

At the office, Harv helped Cal put Silvestra's bike in the trunk. She'd fallen asleep and he didn't disturb her until they were at the Adam's.

"I can walk," she said when he attempted to carry her into the guest house. "Barely," she added, tripping over her own feet.

That did it. Effortlessly, he gathered her up and carried her in.

Solomon's frantic barking could be heard long before they reached the door. When Cal opened it, the dog shot past them.

"Poor thing," Shy said, lying her head on Cal's shoulder. "He's been in all day."

Arms linked around his neck, Shy yawned again and nuzzled his throat with her nose. So overcome with desire, he almost dropped her.

"Where's the bedroom?" He heard the edge in his voice.

"Second room on the right."

She weighed nothing in his arms. As light as a bag of feathers. When Cal turned into the room he was pleased by what he saw, how perfectly the decor fit her. A king-sized bed with brass head and footboards was covered with a quilt he instinctively knew Mabel had made. The dresser, washstand, and stand-up closet were all blond wood, sturdy and handsome. A blue Tiffany lamp sat on the bedside table, alongside it, a picture of Silvestra's son.

"I'm putting you to bed," he said, hoarsely. "You're dead on your feet."

"Mmm."

Cal pulled back the quilt and laid Silvestra down on the sheets. Taking off her shoes, he said, "I want you to rest."

"Mmm."

Silvestra snuggled into the pillow, opened her eyes a fraction, and smiled. Placing the covers over her, Cal bent down and kissed her forehead.

Her sleeping murmur was still in the air as he watched her quickly descend into total oblivion.

Before heading back to town he detoured up to the main house.

"Is she okay?" Mabel asked after he told them what happened.

"She's sleeping now," he said. "Would you—"

"You don't even have to ask, Cal," Jake interrupted. "If I know my wife, the second you drive away, she'll be down there checking on the girl."

Cal sighed and ran his hand through his hair.

"She believes those cattle were killed?" Mabel asked, shaking her head.

"Yes."

"Well, it's true then. Shy has always been able to feel evil, to touch it. The last case she worked on before the -"

She stopped and placed her hand over her mouth.

"Before what?" Cal asked.

"Well, the last case she worked on was a horrible one, let's just say that. From the moment Shy was brought in she could taste the evil surrounding it. She said afterward in some television interview, I think, 'I've met the devil and his name's not Satan. It's Steven Reynolds Smith."

Cal's brow furrowed. "I know that name. He's some sort of pedophile."

"That and a lot more. Working on the case nearly broke Shy in every way: emotionally, physically, and spiritually. She was hospitalized for over three months after it."

"Is that why she's here? She's still recuperating from the strain?"

"That, yes, and some other things, too. Personal things."

Cal thought a moment. "Mabel, why isn't her family with her? Why did she leave her husband, her son, to come here? It doesn't fit with the person I'm beginning to know to leave them behind."

Mabel sighed, her eyes never leaving Cal's face. She wanted to tell him, he could see that. But something stopped her.

"Cal, Shy's a very private person caught in the public's eye and under a lot of scrutiny. If she hasn't confided things to you about her life, don't worry. When she feels the time is right she will. I just don't think it's my place to do so. She's had enough stories written about her over the years, especially last year, to last a lifetime. Stories about her personal life, stories ridiculing her professional one. When she's ready, she'll let you in. Until then, I can't help you. I promised her I wouldn't say anything to anyone here about her."

Cal recognized the gleam in her eyes and the hint she'd thrown him. His grin was wry as he said, "Okay, Mabel. Thanks. Just take care of her until I get back, okay?"

She cocked her head to one side. "You're coming back?"

He planted his hat firmly on his head. "Yes. I have some work to finish up, but I'll be back."

"Cal, the phone's been ringing off the hook for the past three hours. Where have you been?" Harv's exasperation was plain in his voice and the worried concern around his drawn mouth.

Cal strode to his desk, tossed his hat to the rack, on which it landed perfectly, and unholstered his gun.

"Oklahoma City."

"What?" Harv's blue eyes widened as the word exploded from him. "What in hell were you doing there?"

"A little research," he replied.

"Well while you were doing your *research* I've been a telephone answering machine. You've gotten over a dozen messages, half of them from the Lazy Q."

"And the rest?"

"Ben Cambdon's called twice, and the Shelly brothers, Kent Watson and Tara Winslow have all been looking for you. Nate Bolton, too."

"What's going on?" Cal wasn't sure he wanted to hear why all the major cattle ranchers in the area had been trying to get in touch with him.

Harv sighed heavily and ran his meaty hands through thinning, graying hair. "Seems Amos Pierce has been broadcasting all over Renewal and the abutting counties about Silvestra Coeltrain and what she can do."

"It's not a side-show trick, Harv. It's the way she's made."

"Don't jump down my throat. I'm not the one who's ridiculing her."

Cal lowered his eyes, annoyed he'd snapped at his Deputy. "Sorry. Go on."

Collecting himself, Harv said, "The ranchers want to have a meeting. Here. Tonight."

"About what?"

"What do you think? Those dead cows. Amos has convinced everyone there's some crazed cattle killer targeting them all. First Ben Cambdon loses three, then he loses ten. He wants you to do something about it before it goes any further. And he wants Mrs. Coeltrain in on it."

"What does he expect us to do? I've got a staff of four, for Pete's sake."

"That's what they're all coming here to discuss. Nine o'clock. Sharp, according to Amos."

"And all the other calls are related to this?"

"Yeah."

"Rand Denny call in anything yet?"

Harv checked the message sheets. "No. Last I heard, he had the Pierce cattle transported to the clinic and was gonna start slicing'em up."

Cal leaned back in his chair, feet up on the desk, crossed at the ankles. Steepling his fingers, he said, "Okay. Let'em come. I'll be here. You'd better call Sherry and tell her you'll be busy after supper for a while."

"Already did. She wasn't pleased."

He didn't sound so, either, Cal thought.

After a few minutes of thoughtful silence, Harv asked, "So what was so God awful important you drove all the way to Oklahoma City?"

Cal stared at him, debating about what and how much he should reveal. Reluctantly, he decided to keep his information close.

"Can't tell you right now, Harv. But it was an important trip for me that came up sudden-like. I needed to get some information we didn't have the capacity to find out here."

"Even with this hi-tech junk the City Council donated?" he asked, flicking a finger at the computer.

Cal laughed for the first time in hours. He knew the sarcasm in his deputy's voice was warranted. The computer had already been obsolete when the council bought it - second hand - eighteen months before. Hoping to upgrade the information gathering, cataloging, and reporting of the Sheriff's office had been their altruistic goal. Unfortunately, more times than not, the system went down right in the middle of a job.

"Our hi-tech junk, as you so lovingly call it, wasn't able to tell me what I needed to know. I used the computer at the Police Crime lab in O.C. Called in a favor from Bob McGregor."

Harv studied the Sheriff. "For you to drive an hour each way and then call in a favor from the Chief of Police tells me you've been on a mission."

Cal nodded. "You could say that. Listen, why don't you go home and get something to eat. Be back around eight-thirty, okay?"

"Fine with me." Harv holstered his gun, put on his hat, and headed for the door.

"Tell Sherry hello and that I'm sorry you're going to be working late."

"She doesn't mind, really. Well, not too much," he said, smiling.

Alone with his thoughts, Cal replayed everything he'd learned that afternoon. The impromptu trip, the idea of which had been planted by Mabel Adams in a quest to find out more about Silvestra, had proved highly informative. Bob McGregor was surprised to see Cal, but their professional friendship was an old and solid one. He'd been quickly granted the use of their system and Cal went to work. He typed in Silvestra's name and requested all references to her for the past seven years.

There were plenty.

Cal learned she'd worked on over five dozen missing person cases, all children, and had a success rate of ninety-eight percent in locating them. Unfortunately, about one-third of the children were found dead.

There were a few interviews concerning specific cases, and a feature article in PEOPLE magazine about her, her psychic work, and her book series. She'd been called everything from a genius to a quack; made the society pages of the Boston and New York papers twice. Once detailing her marriage to Dr. Paul Coeltrain, her former therapist, and the second on the birth of her son, Giovanni.

Cal studied the grainy newspaper photograph of the bride and groom on the screen. Neither of them appeared at ease. Silvestra's smile was forced, her forehead wrinkled. The good Dr. Coeltrain's face was pallid, the smile, little more than a smirk. Jealousy bubbled and boiled within the Sheriff again as he read how the bride and groom had known each other for nine years, ever since she'd come to him as a patient.

Why would a ten-year-old need a therapist? And what kind of doctor allows himself to fall in love with a client?

Cal meant to find out.

He called up the final articles on Silvestra - the Steven Reynolds Smith case.

Shy'd been called in by the police in New York when three children, all boys from five-to-seven years old, were discovered missing from the same block of a small, rural upstate town. Before the case was completed, four more boys had disappeared. In an interview Silvestra told of being stymied from the start. Usually, clothing or personal items from the victims would help her get a read on the location, or help her fixate on the victim's mind set. But with this case, every feeling, every inclination she got was futile in locating the boys. She felt like a failure, especially when the other boys vanished. It wasn't until the last kidnapping, though, she was able to zero in on something. The person responsible for the disappearances had left behind a valuable clue: one worn, old sneaker from the latest victim.

When Silvestra touched the shoe, she immediately sensed total and complete life. She realized then why her other leads hadn't panned out - the victims had been killed instantly. This last one, the killer had plans for.

Silvestra's powers keyed into the sneaker and a vision flashed in her mind. A neon sign that blinked twenty-four hours a day. Loud music, trash cans overturning, and the chemical stench of formaldehyde.

From the physical description, the police staked out a seedy section of town and found the bar with the blinking sign. A set of apartments sat atop it. A conversation with the landlord turned up information on a new tenant, there for just one month. His hallway smelled strong, like a hospital, the landlord stated, but he'd been paid for six months' rent in advance, so he asked no questions.

The police stormed the apartment after Silvestra confirmed the scene was the one in her vision. What they found horrified everyone from the police down to the parents of the missing children.

As Cal read the report of the gruesome acts Smith had committed on the boys, he agreed with Shy's statement that the man was the devil.

He flipped the cursor and the screen showed one more article, one Cal hadn't expected. As he read through it, anger flowed through him. He read it twice just to make sure he'd gotten it right. Cal sat there a full ten minutes, letting the information seep in. His anger quickly grew to empathy and then hurt.

He was going to know why she'd lied to him.

Alighting from the car back at the Adams' he heard the sound of music drifting on the breeze. Cal didn't recognize the melody, but getting closer to the guesthouse, realized he wouldn't have. It was a classical piece, deep tones filled with power, with pain, being played with a force he found seductive, enticing.

The front door stood ajar. With mild trepidation, he pushed it open and found her seated at the old upright piano. Her body swayed back and forth, her hands reached out, caressing the keys with the melody as a lover would caress a cheek.

No sheet music sat in front of her.

Suddenly, the music changed, grew louder, fiercer, more passionate. Silvestra's upper body careened violently side to side as her hands reached, struck keys and then reached further. Cal's midsection trembled as she pounded out the last movement, her arms flying across the keyboard.

At the last chord, her hands came down, then up, and she leaned into the piano, depleted, spent. He watched her breathing return to normal.

The room echoed with the resonating sound of the piece she'd played.

When all grew quiet, Cal watched her sit upright, message a neck kink and then stretch. He stood rooted to the floor, overcome with the emotions surging through him which the music, and the woman, evoked.

Silvestra turned. Cal watched scared surprise turn to delight on her face.

"I didn't know you were there." Her eyes raked over his face, down his body.

"The door was open. I didn't knock, didn't want to disturb you."

Shy smiled.

"You play beautifully, Silvestra. I've never heard anyone make an old upright sound like a Steinway."

His heart skipped a beat when a pleased blush spread up her face.

"Thank you."

"How long have you played?"

She shrugged. "Always. I don't remember a time when I didn't, couldn't. Sometimes, my music has been the only friend I've had. I'm glad you're here," she said, closing the distance between them. "I want to talk to you about something. Sit down, please," she said.

Cal saw her link her fingers, unlink them again, and then place them in the pockets of her skirt. He realized she was nervous.

He put up a hand. "Wait. There's something important I have to say first."

Silvestra swallowed, sighed. "Okay. Go ahead."

"I drove to Oklahoma City this afternoon after I dropped you off. I had a little research to do?"

"On what?"

"You. I wanted, really, to find out about some of the cases you've worked on."

"And did you?"

"Yes. More than I bargained for. A few things surprised me," he said, watching her face. "One, that you'd married your therapist, and the other, that your son and husband are dead."

The accusation, for that's what it was, hung in the air like a bad odor.

"You've never answered my questions about why you're here and your family is thousands of miles away. I thought it might be because you're going through a divorce, but then, why would you leave your son? It never crossed my mind they were dead. You lied to me, Silvestra. Why?"

"Technically, I didn't lie," she said, then added quickly when he squinted, "but I won't argue semantics with you. I'll admit, though, that you weren't told the complete truth about me."

In one brief move, he crossed to her and grabbed her upper arms. "Dammit, Silvestra, don't play games with me. I think I have a right to know."

"All right," she whispered. "You can let me go."

He pulled back and ran his hands through his hair. He sat and Silvestra stood behind the love seat opposite him.

"Actually, that you already know may make this easier. I've been mulling over all afternoon about how I was going to tell you."

Cal recognized the hesitation in her eyes and his anger began to dissipate. Settling back on the couch, one leg crossed over the other, he said, "I'm listening."

She took a deep breath, held it a second, and then let it out. "From the first day we met, I think it would be honest to say we've been attracted to one another."

He raised one eyebrow in a questioning slant.

"Okay. Maybe more than just attracted. You were under the assumption I was married and since I was introduced to you as Mrs. Coeltrain, I can see how you'd believe it. I'm a very private person, despite the fact I help the public. I've always tried to keep my personal life just that. When I arrived, I asked Mabel and Jake to keep quiet about the reason I was here. I didn't want people staring, talking behind their backs, or asking me millions of questions about my psychic abilities, which is what most people naturally do when they find out. I just wanted some rest, quiet. To get away from, well, from bad memories."

"Mabel said you'd been ill the past year."

"Ill? Well, yes I guess you could say I was. Both physically and mentally. The last missing person case I worked on -"

"The Smith case."

Her brows furrowed.

Cal shrugged. "I read about it Oklahoma City. Mabel mentioned it in passing, and said it had taken a great toll on you."

Shy's laugh held no warmth or amusement. "That's the understatement of the year. Yes, it took a great toll on me. But not only because the case was horribly exhausting. It affected my personal life in a way no other case ever had."

He watched her pace about the room, all nervous energy and movement.

Abruptly, she stopped and turned to face him. He saw her swallow again, her eyes growing wet.

"I have to tell you this," she said.

Cal wondered who she was trying to convince more.

She turned and sat back down. "You know about the case itself, so I won't go over it. I hadn't seen my husband or my son in over a month. They were staying in Boston so Giovanni could go to school. He loved it so much, I hated pulling him out just to have him with me when I worked. Paul agreed to stay home and I went to New York. When the police finally found Smith, I wasn't needed any longer. I decided to catch an earlier flight home, back to Boston. I missed Giovanni so much and I was so tired from the mental strain of the case, I just wanted to go home and sleep in my own bed. I booked a flight and was at the terminal when...it happened."

Her color turned to chalk. Her bottom lip trembled, and she averted her eyes, closing them, as if wiping out the memory. He leaned forward and took her hand. Shocked, he found them ice cold. "Silvestra, don't -"

"No." Her eyes flew open. "I have to. I have to talk about it. It's the only way the pain will ever go away. I know that now."

Watching the despair grow across her face, his heart wrenched. Keeping her hands, he said softly, "Go on, then."

She wet parched lips with a flick of her tongue. "It seems Paul had heard on the television news Smith had been arrested. He knew my job was over and he wanted to surprise me. He booked a private plane to bring them down to New York to meet me. He didn't call."

"So, you were both on your way to surprise the other."

"Yes. I was at the airport, waiting to board my plane when my hands went cold and numb. I sat back and let the vision come. It was of Paul and Gio. They were on a plane. It was...burning... the fire was...everywhere. I could hear Gio calling for me...screaming 'Mama, Mama!' over and over. Then, a black explosion burst in my brain."

"*Jesus.*"

"I jumped up and ran to the ticket counter. I told them who I was, what I thought was going to happen. They gave me the runaround, thought I was some psycho. Finally, I started screaming so loudly, they called the airport supervisor. Luckily, he'd seen my picture on the news and recognized me.

I was able to convince him of what was going to happen. He radioed the Boston air control and told them about the plane my husband was on. But it was too late to cancel it, it had departed ten minutes prior to the call. Just as the air traffic controller was radioing the cockpit, they heard a distress call. It was Paul's plane. They could hear screaming, yelling, confusion. Then, an explosion and nothing."

Shy stopped and dragged in a breath.

"They found the wreckage the next day. Of course, there were no survivors. I lost both of them."

He'd known about the accident. It had been the last article in the computer profile. The article, though, had been logical, rational, precise in language and detail. To hear Silvestra tell the story, to hear the anguish and suffering her voice gave forth, killed him inside. To loose all that you love, all that means anything to you, at one time was devastating. His arms tightened around her.

Shy rested her head on his shoulder, sniffed. "I was in the hospital for three months after that. At the time I worked on the Smith case, I'd been pregnant. Paul hadn't known. I was going to tell him after I got home. He worried so much about me, too much sometimes. I..." her voice faltered. "I...lost the baby from the shock...a little girl."

"Dear God." Cal's voice broke.

"It was...too much to handle. Too much grief at one time. All I wanted to do was die. I blamed myself. If I hadn't been working so hard, devoting all my time, all my energy to the case, they would still be alive."

He laid his chin on to the top of her head and sighed.

"Silvestra, you can't think that," he said at last. "None of what happened was your fault. None of it."

"I know that now, or at least I'm beginning to," she said. "My parents came to see me in the hospital. They said the same thing, that I wasn't to blame. But their grief was as great as mine. They loved Gio with all their hearts. They were the ones who suggested I come and spend some time with Mabel and Jake. When I was strong enough, I decided to."

Pulling completely away from him, Shy sat upright. Wiping her nose with the back of her hand, she continued. "When I first arrived I had nightmares every night. Mabel told me they could hear me screaming up at the house."

"What were they about?"

She shivered and he wanted to pull her back. When she crossed her arms, Cal let her be, knowing that was what she needed.

"I heard a young boy's voice wailing, screaming for me to help him. I couldn't figure out if was one of the boys Smith had murdered, or if ..."

"It was Giovanni," he finished.

"Yes. Can you understand how helpless I felt when I had the power to save him and couldn't? Do you know what that does to me, his mother, to know my child died and I couldn't prevent it?"

Cal heard the hysteria creeping into her voice. Forgetting what she wanted and needed, he thrust forward and dragged her up, shaking her roughly. "Stop it! Just stop it, Silvestra. Castigating yourself like this does no good. What happened is a tragedy, yes, but you are blameless. You can't go on for the rest of your life condemning yourself. You have to move ahead, beyond the pain, past the hurt. You have to start living again."

Shy's eyes flew open wide with the jarring.

The room grew quiet, dead quiet. They both stood, staring at the other.

Slowly, Cal's hands released her. "I'm sorry," he said. "I have no right."

"You told me you wanted me even though I was another man's wife."

He squinted. "Yes, I did. I meant it. I hated myself for feeling it, but I meant it."

"Do you still, now that you know I'm not? Now that you know I deceived you, led you to believe something that wasn't true?"

Her eyes turned to smoke. They bore into his with such heat, such intensity. In answer, Cal took a step closer, forcing her head back to continue looking at him. Cautiously, with the gentleness he'd been lacking moments ago, Cal took her in his arms and said, voice soft as a whisper, "I want you more than any woman or anything I've ever wanted in my life. And not just in my bed. I can't stop thinking about you, about us, together, about how it would be. You're the most amazing woman I've ever met. A contradiction. Soft and feminine, you look like you could break if I so much as blew on you. But underneath that silky exterior, you're all fire. The few times we've kissed, I've felt the heat bounce out of you, the strength. I don't know any woman who could have gone through what you did and survive. I don't know any woman who could do what you do, face the things you face, and retain such an untouched, pure nature."

Silvestra's gaze never wavered from his.

"You're the most amazing woman I've ever met. And the sexiest," he added, the corners of his full lips twitching upward. "You churn things up in me that I never thought any woman could. You make me feel, Silvestra, really feel, deep inside, in my soul. I want to be with you. I want to be inside of you. I want all of you, every last bit you can give. Do you understand that?"

Cal's lips sought hers hungrily, starved for the feel of her, the taste. Silvestra met him with the same ravenous passion and need. He felt her release when she arched, clawing her hands up his torso, clinging, clutching as if her life, her very essence depended on it.

Suddenly he pulled back, needing to see her face, to see what was in her eyes, the mirrors to her mind.

And he did.

"Silvestra," he whispered against lips that touched her eyes, nuzzled her brow. "I can't make what happened in your life go away. But I know you've touched me as no woman ever has. I know this is right; meant to be. I need to hear you say you want me as much as I do you."

"I do," Shy said quickly. "That's why I had to tell you the truth. I couldn't have it between us, having you feel guilty for wanting something you thought you had no right to."

Smoothing the crease in her brow, Cal let his hand cup her chin. Her amber eyes were warm gold, all heat radiating from within. The pale, drawn face he'd seen moments before was now flushed, the skin feverish, silky.

"Stay with me," she said.

The request, so simply made, yet telling him everything he wanted to know, drove him to the brink.

In one fluid motion, Cal lifted her up and moved toward the bedroom. Silvestra's head lolled against his shoulder and he could feel her breath, hot and fast on his neck.

With one knee bent on the bed for support, Cal placed Shy across the eyelet quilt. Her eyes were liquid gold, red-hot fire burning from the centers like an active volcano. She held out her arms and he drifted into them. Lying hip to hip, their hands began traveling, exploring, while their eyes stayed locked.

"Silvestra," Cal whispered, leaning in for a kiss. "I want this to be perfect."

She traced a finger across his lips and murmured, "It already is."

Cal pressed her back against the bed, covering her mouth. Heat, searing heat engulfed him. When his tongue teased her lips and they parted on the invitation, Cal's whole body exploded in a blaze of rapture. Never had a woman tasted so sweet and so exotic at the same time. All his concentration centered on her mouth and the exquisite texture of it. The mole peeking from the corner proved too enticing to ignore. Pulling back to look at it, he traced a finger along the delicate and tiny imperfection that was so perfect on her.

"I love this mole." When his tongue flicked across it, gently sucked at the little growth, Silvestra arched, groaned.

Smiling, Cal stared down at her face. Eyes half-closed, a delicious and feline smile spread across ruby lips, she looked more beautiful, more enticing than anything he'd ever seen.

With one hand gently cupping her breast through the fabric of her simple shirt, Cal traced his thumb along the center, rewarded immediately by the feel of her nipple hardening. He couldn't wait, had to see her, feel her skin against his. Roughly, with hands trembling with desire, he undid the shirt buttons.

Pushing aside the flimsy material of her bra, Cal held one perfect breast in his naked hand. Her skin was alive, warm, vibrant. Velvety smooth, yet firm and youthful. When his lips brushed across the swollen nub, his tongue wetting it, tasting, savoring, Silvestra called out his name, fisting his hair.

"Shush, darlin'," he said, coming up for another kiss. "Relax. Let me love you."

As an answer, she cupped the back of his head, brought it down, and hungrily devoured his mouth.

Spurred on by her response, Cal lifted her and removed the rest of her clothing.

Cal could see the outline of her rib cage when his fingers traced across the tiny waist. His mouth did a slow dance down the column of her throat, across the swell of beautiful ripe breasts, navel. The small scar cutting across her lower abdomen was a surprise. He kissed it carefully, recognizing at once what it was.

Silvestra writhed beneath him. Beams of light shot behind his eyes as his mouth covered every inch of her skin.

This was heaven, it had to be. Nothing on earth could feel this wonderful, this exhilarating, this incredibly delicious.

Snaking her hand into the collar of his shirt, she popped the buttons from top to bottom. Yanking it out of his waistband, her hands splayed across his chest, kneading, investigating. The whimper that came from the back of her throat thrilled him.

Deft fingers gingerly undid the belt, then the zipper of his pants. When her hands reached in, cupped his buttocks, kneading the flesh, pressing him closer to her, Cal could barely control the eruption quaking his insides.

"*God*, Silvestra." He threw off his clothes until they both were naked.

One hand traced the gentle swell of her mound, while his mouth did delectable things to her lips. When he tracked a finger between her thighs, felt her pulsing, wet, ready for him, Cal had to check every ounce of will he had not to ram into her, take her with the riot and need sprinting through his body. When she reached out a hand and chaliced him, stroking back and forth, Cal knew what it meant to die a slow, torpid death.

"Silvestra, no," he said, pulling her hand away. When she looked up at him, he saw the question in her eyes. "I want to play for a while," he said, pushing her back down on the mattress. "I want to know every inch of you."

With his mouth, he discovered all the parts that made her a woman. His tongue discovered places so erotic, so sensual, her limbs went slack beneath him. And when his mouth found that small, delicate spot pulsing with the heat of longing, she screamed his name, arched, hips bucking under the gentle sucking.

When the waves calmed, Silvestra opened her eyes to find him smiling above her.

He'd taken her far, but they still had miles to go.

"I want you inside me," she said, her voice raspy, filled with craving. "I need to feel you inside me. Now."

She grasped him again, her fingers gently massaging, tugging. She rubbed the moisture she found on his tip then spread it down his shaft and back up again.

"Shy -" He couldn't breathe, couldn't think. All he could do was feel. When she had him almost to the ledge, almost ready to jump, his mind cleared.

"Look at me," he commanded. Her eyes flew open and for the first time in his life, Cal knew what real love looked like.

In one liquid motion, he entered, heard her gasp, then quake beneath him.

"Cal! Cal! You're so -"

"Shush, darlin'...let me... just let me fill you slowly."

God, she was so small he thought she might break. Her walls tightened around him and when he looked down, Cal knew it wasn't pain across her face, but pure female ecstasy.

Slowly, gently, at first, he began to rock, pulling her legs over his hips, vesseling her buttocks in his hands. Soon, the cadence changed, both of them fighting for a control that wouldn't last.

When Cal felt her tighten, convulse around him, heard his name called again, he lost all control and gave himself up, a willing prisoner to both their primal needs.

His breathing slowed, but his heart still pounded like a drumline.

Silvestra shifted beneath him and he pulled back on his elbows in time to see her face before she turned away from him. Small, fragile tears wet her lashes.

Guilt hammered at his heart. He'd been too rough, too demanding. God, she was still so fragile, so delicate and he'd taken her like an animal.

"Silvestra, I'm sorry," he whispered, voice catching. He laid his head down on hers, brow to brow.

"Why?" she asked after a few moments.

"I hurt you, I didn't mean to, I -"

"You didn't hurt me, Cal. Quite the opposite, in fact."

When he opened his eyes he found her half-smile. "But you're crying. I thought I -"

Silvestra placed a finger across his lips. "I'm not hurt. That's not why I'm crying. It's just -."

"Tell me, please."

A soft blush spread up her neck and face. "It's never been, well...I've never felt such...release before. That's never happened to me. It felt wonderful."

Cal's heart melted. "Never?"

"Never."

The force that shot through his system electrified Cal with a surge of delight. That she'd been married, had a child, didn't seem to exist any longer. She was his; his alone. He'd given her a gift so precious, so priceless, he immediately felt humbled, honored.

Gently he brought his lips to hers. "I love you, Silvestra."

Cal saw the confusion melt over her face and felt a small tear of hurt rip in his heart. Quickly, he shrugged it off. The words may not be there for her yet, but he knew she loved him. He could feel it, could taste it on her. She was afraid to tell him, afraid of what it might change, what it might bring. This, Cal could understand. The hurt eased away, replaced by acceptance.

She'd tell him soon enough.

Until then, they were here together.

Silvestra's hand trailed up and down his back, her nails gently grating his tanned skin. He went hard in an instant.

Trailing a line of kisses and nibbles along her neck, he confessed, "I don't seem to be able to get enough of you."

Silvestra wrapped her arms around his neck and laughed. "I'm yours, Sheriff. Take all you want."

Before his mouth seared to hers again, he drawled, "It'll be my pleasure, ma'am."

Chapter Nine

Cal slowly ascended into consciousness.

Silvestra was lying across him, one leg seductively twined with his.

The past few hours had been magical. Every fantasy he'd had about Silvestra didn't hold a candle to the real thing. They'd shared their bodies, their spirits. Cal didn't know why he'd ever thought this woman fragile or delicate. She was a mountain of strength, giving back everything she received in full measure, taking him places he'd never been, nor dreamed of reaching.

I've lost more than my heart, he thought, absently rubbing her neck. I've lost my soul as well.

"Are you awake?" he asked.

"Barely."

When she lifted her head and regarded him with a smile, her sleepy eyes were half-open. "I had the most wonderful dream. *Oh.* I guess it wasn't a dream after all," she added, rising on an elbow.

Cal's lips twitched. Weaving a hand through her hair he kissed the smile.

"I'm dreaming again," she said, her head returning to its resting place.

Running his fingers down her arm, he caught sight of the time on the clock next to the bed. It was already eight-thirty. "I have to go."

"Why?" she asked, nuzzling his chest with her nose. When he explained the reason, she sat up. "I want to go with you."

Cal could see the steely determination in her eyes. He sat on the edge of the bed and began dressing. "No," he said. "I want to handle this my way. This isn't a witch hunt, Silvestra, and I won't have it turned into one by Amos Pierce. He's spooked enough by this whole situation. I don't know what the other ranchers have been told about you."

When he stood to slip into his pants, Silvestra wrapped the sheet around her, sari-like, and sat in the spot Cal had vacated. "But if I come, maybe I can dispel some of their fears."

He shook his head, mouth firm. "No. I mean it."

"Will you come back and tell me about what happened?"

Cal yanked her up from the bed and surrounded her with his arms. "Nothing could keep me away," he said, crushing his lips to hers. "Nothing."

They walked to the door together, Silvestra still wrapped in the sheet. From the living room, Solomon's head rose for a second, stared at them, and then lolled back onto the carpet, asleep instantly.

Cal looked down at the woman his heart now belonged to, and gathered her into the fullness of his embrace. Tipping her head back, he kissed her one last time.

"I'll be back as soon as I can."

"I'll be waiting," she told him.

The Sheriff wasn't pleased to see his office turned into a town meeting hall. The moment he walked into the station he was accosted from all angles by angry and worried ranchers.

It took him a few minutes to quiet them all down.

"I understand Amos Pierce called you all together," he said, finally having their undivided attention.

"That I did, Sheriff." Amos stepped forward. "I let 'em know what happened out at my place today."

"Ten healthy head of cattle all dying together like that isn't natural," Tara Winslow said. "Especially when you add Ben's loss in, too."

Cal looked down at the rancher's sun wrinkled face with its shock of short gray hair, into crystal clear blue eyes. "You know something I don't Tara?"

"What d'ya mean?"

"Last I heard it hadn't been determined the animals died from the same cause. Has Rand Denny come to that conclusion?"

Tara's eyes turned to Amos. "You said they were the same. Is it true, or not?"

Cal evaluated the controlled ire she'd directed at her neighboring rancher and knew he never wanted to be on the cutting edge of that anger.

"Far as I know, Denny hasn't figured out yet why or how they died," Amos reluctantly answered. "But that young woman you had with you today, Cal, she said they'd been killed. All my men heard her." Indignant, he squared his shoulders.

"Who is this woman, Sheriff, and why would she say something like that?" Dayton Sherry asked.

"Amos said she claimed to be some kind of psychic who worked with the police in New York," his brother Daniel added. "Is it true?"

Questions flew at Cal again concerning Silvestra. He put his hands up and asked them all to quiet down. It was a full minute before the room grew silent again.

Quickly, yet thoroughly, Cal explained who Silvestra was and how she'd been known to help the police. The faces surrounding him were skeptical at best. In one corner, he noticed Priscilla and Ethan Bolton deep in whispered conversation, their heads together and bowed.

"Now, if Mrs. Coeltrain says she feels Amos' cattle were killed, then I'd bet money they were," Cal said, eyeing every rancher. "But just because someone targeted the Lazy Q, doesn't mean the rest of you are at any kind of risk."

"How do you explain Ben's cattle, then?" Daniel asked. "What does this Mrs. Coeltrain think about them?"

"She hasn't indicated to me or anyone else those cattle died by the same hand or in the same way."

"But she *did* know about them," Ben said from his leaning position against Cal's desk. "Didn't she?"

Confronted by Ben's deduction, Cal nodded. "She'd had a vision, similar to the one about Amos' herd."

"That would explain," Ben said, crossing his arms, "how you both came to be at my ranch right after the animals were discovered."

"Yes."

The room grew deathly still.

"What exactly do we know about this woman, Cal?" Priscilla asked, coming forward.

Cal's mouth tightened into a thin, hard, line. "Pris?"

"Well," she said, licking her lips, turning to eye every man in the room. "She comes to town, no one knows her except the Adams', and then all of a sudden cattle start dying. Remember, we lost one, too, and this Coeltrain woman was the one to find it. Who's to say she isn't responsible for these deaths?"

Hands fisted at his sides, Cal's face grew tight and closed. "Have a care, Pris," he said through clenched teeth. "You don't want to be accused of slandering someone." The words stuck in his throat and came out sounding more like a threat than a warning.

Priscilla would not be put off. Tossing ginger curls with defiance, she said, "Well, who's to say she isn't responsible? All we have is her word these animals have been killed. Rand hasn't come up with anything yet. Maybe she did it."

"Why would she kill our cattle, girl? It doesn't make sense."

Priscilla's green eyes glared at her father, fury laced in them. "I don't know, Daddy," she said, swiping a hand across her hair. "Maybe she wants attention. Maybe she's just plum crazy. Maybe she gets off on killing things and then making believe she has these visions so she'll look like some kind of hero. You hear about wacky people like this every day."

Cal had heard enough. "I'd shut my mouth right now if I was you, Priscilla Bolton. You're digging a hole way bigger than even you can crawl out of."

There was a cutting edge of danger in his voice. It told everyone in the room exactly whose side the Sheriff was on.

Barely an arm's distance from him, hands on hips, she sneered. "If you'd stop thinking with what's in your pants and start thinking with your head you'd realize I'm making sense."

Lips pulled back in a snarl of frenzy, Cal advanced on her.

Whatever would have happened next was stopped by Harv pulling Cal in one direction, Ethan yanking his sister in the opposite. Nathanial stepped between them. "Enough. This isn't getting us anywhere."

Cal tried to get a grip on his anger, but just looking at Priscilla made it more than difficult. He wanted to take her over his knee and deliver the spanking she'd deserved since childhood.

"She has no cause to say those things about Mrs. Coeltrain, Nate. It's slander and spite, pure and simple," Harv said.

"I agree." Turning to his children, face stern and lips pinched, Nathanial said, "Go on home. I've had enough of the two of you for one night."

"But Daddy -" Priscilla pulled against her brother's restraining hand.

"I said git, girl!"

Eyes blazing, Pris threw the Sheriff a look of pure loathing, yanked away from Ethan and stormed from the room, all eyes following her back.

Cal faced Ethan, whose own green eyes fixed the Sheriff with a level stare. Scowling, he said, "Don't ever touch her again, Blackbear, or you'll be six feet under before you can blink."

"Threatening an officer of the law can get you incarcerated, son," Harv said sternly, his free hand fingering his gun holster.

Lips curling backward, Ethan's eyes stayed glued to Cal. "Touching my sister can get a man killed," he said, his voice thick, dripping with hatred.

"That's enough, boy." Nate roared. "Get home. Follow your sister."

The room, dense with tension, cleared some as the young man blew out the door.

Nate turned to the Sheriff and his Deputy. "I'm sorry. I don't know what's gotten into those two lately. Been as nervous and jumpy as two June brides."

Cal's anger slowly dissolved, checked by the responsibility he bore for the badge.

"All this is fine and dandy, but I've still got ten dead head of cattle," Amos blared. "What are you gonna do about it, Sheriff?"

"There's not much I can do, Amos, to be truthful. I can put Pete on overtime duty, have him stake out your ranch at night if you want, but he doesn't know the terrain like your men do. If you're really worried, if any of you are, that something's going to happen to your livestock, I'd say post men in shifts around your property."

Amos glared at the other ranchers. "Doesn't sound like too bad an idea," he said, grudgingly.

"Not at all," Tara agreed.

For the next few minutes, they all spoke together, devising plans for their cowhands to oversee the ranch at different times and shifts throughout the day and night. Cal and Harv volunteered to help if it was needed.

When the last of the ranchers had gone, Cal sat at his desk, head cradled in his hands.

"Losin' it with Pris Bolton wasn't exactly the smartest thing I've ever seen you do," Harv said.

Cal's laugh had a biting, bitter ring to it. "You won't get any argument from me."

The phone rang. "It's Rand," Harv said, handing Cal the receiver.

"Blackbear."

"I just finished a preliminary exam on Pierce's cattle."

"And?"

"There's something interesting in my findings."

"I'll be right there."

The Sheriff grabbed his hat from the rack.

"Important?" Harv asked.

"Could be. Why'nt you go on home. I'll call if I need you."

Cal sped left at Main street and was at the clinic in less than two minutes. Finding the front door unlocked, he walked in.

"That you, Cal?" Rand called.

"Yeah."

"Come on back. I'm in the O.R."

Cal worked his way down the unlit corridor to the back of the clinic. He found Rand standing over a steel table, a vivisected cow atop it. The vet was garbed in a plastic apron, his hands sheathed in blue rubber gloves. Across his face, a pair of plastic goggles protected his eyes. At present, he was weighing something on a scale suspended from the ceiling.

"So what's so interesting?" the Sheriff asked.

Rand made a notation on a clipboard before replying. "Remember I told you Ben Cambdon's cows had enlarged hearts?"

Cal squinted. "Yeah. You said it's not uncommon when the animal's up in years."

"That's true. But Amos' cattle here are all barely two years old. Even though they've been fattened up for auction, their hearts shouldn't be enlarged."

"Are they?"

"Have a look for yourself."

He stepped back from the scale and Cal saw an enormous, bright red mass sitting in it. "What exactly am I looking at?"

"This heart's from the third cow I've opened. The other two look exactly the same: swollen atriums, bulging ventricles. That's not normal in an animal this age. Ben's cattle had the same kind of findings, but his were older by a few years, so I attributed it to age."

"But now you're not sure?"

"No. No, I'm not." Rand removed the goggles and gloves, wiped his eyes with the pads of his thumbs.

"What would cause something like this?" Cal asked. "Is it that mad cow disease or something like it?"

Rand shook his head. "No, in those cases the cattle all had neurotoxicity."

When Cal stared at him mutely, Rand explained. "The disease affects the central nervous system specifically. I saw no evidence of that in these cattle. It's all cardiovascular in context."

"So what would cause it?"

"I'm not sure. Any number of things, I imagine. If I had to make a guess, though, speculate on a cause, I'd say some kind of chemical intervention."

"What?"

Rand looked Cal squarely in the eyes. "This is just between you and me, but I'd hazard a guess these animals were given something, some chemical or drug to cause their systems to rapidly speed up and overwork their hearts in some way. That's the reason I think the organs are enlarged. They were grossly overtaxed."

Cal thought for a moment. "Are you saying these cows, what? Had heart attacks?"

"To put it simply, yes."

"And you think that's been caused by some kind of chemical?"

"If I had to guess, yes."

"How can you know for sure?"

"In Ben's case, I drew off some fluids and sent them to Oklahoma City for analysis. I'll do the same with these animals, but I'm going to bring along the hearts as well. I'll deliver the samples myself and put a rush on the results."

Cal was silent, remembering what occurred at the Lazy Q that afternoon, especially Silvestra's statement.

As if reading his mind, Rand said, "It seems Silvestra Coeltrain may have been right. Something may have been deliberately done to these cows."

"There's no possibility their grain is contaminated, or their water? Nothing like that would cause this?"

"Of course it would. But we'd see total destruction of herds, not isolated, small incidents as we have."

"This doesn't make a whole lot of sense, you know," Cal said. "Who would want to kill these animals? Why?"

"I wish I knew. If this is being done intentionally, though, the other ranchers in the area need to be notified."

"They already have." Cal told him about the meeting.

"If I'm right and these animals have been poisoned, those ranchers have reason to be worried."

"It sounds bizarre," Cal said, leaning against a table, Sheriff's hat tipped way back. "Why would someone want to kill cattle, and in such small quantities? Both ranches have a fair number of head. To lose such a small amount doesn't do anything to them financially."

"Don't let Amos hear you say that."

"It just doesn't make sense."

"Well, that's why they pay you the big Sheriff bucks, Cal. You get to figure these things out. Now, I'd better finish up. I'll drive to Oklahoma City first thing in the morning."

Cal left the man to his work.

It was after eleven, but surprisingly he wasn't tired.

Driving, Cal tried to make sense of what Denny'd told him. The only evidence, if he could call it that, for believing the cattle were intentionally killed was Silvestra's statement. He didn't doubt her for a second. If she believed the animals had been slaughtered, that was good enough for him.

Silvestra.

His mind turned from business to pleasure. Calling her face to mind instantly relaxed him. Cal felt his limbs grow fluid, the knots in his neck and back, work themselves out.

She did that for him. Put him at ease, calmed him when nothing else could.

Most of his life he'd been stuck in a state of tension so thick at times as to almost strangle him. It had started with his birth. Considered an outcast by society, he'd fought hard and long for acceptance in every facet of life, including race. He'd been jeered and teased as a child, come home with a bloodied nose, and torn clothing in high school. It had been easier for Rose. Cal had paved the way, taken most of the racial heat. He hadn't dated until out of college. All the girls he'd liked considered him below them socially. As an adult, he'd found tolerance for his skills, analytical mind, and in the fair way he treated everyone.

But with Silvestra, Cal could relax for the first time, because in her he felt a real, total, and unquestioning acceptance for who and what he was.

And in that acceptance, Cal knew he'd also found love.

Love.

Had he ever allowed himself to feel real love before? He loved his family, of course, but that was different. This feeling surging through him for Silvestra was stronger, more real, more substantial than anything he'd ever allowed himself to feel before.

In Shy, Cal saw equal parts of himself: stubborn, proud, not accepted for things that made them different from others. He realized now he'd recognized the kinship between them from the first day. They were like two halves of a circle, incomplete without the other. Yin and Yang. Man and Woman.

With Silvestra, for the first time, Cal thought of commitment, of continuity. Rose had been lucky to find a man who loved and accepted her and she'd grabbed him fast and held on strong. Cal intended to do the same with Silvestra. Her past was a sad one, true, but he would help her get over the pain, the loss, and build a future together with her, for her.

Thinking about her, Cal turned the squad left when he came to the end of Main Street.

There was really only one place for him to go and it wasn't his secluded, lonely, and empty bachelor apartment.

As soon as Silvestra heard his car she tore through the front door and threw herself into his arms before he was at the threshold.

"I've been so worried," she said, holding him fast.

Cal hugged her tight. "Come on, let's go in and I'll tell you about it."

The living room was bathed in candlelight and an orange glow from the fire she'd lit. They sat together on the loveseat, Cal's arm over her shoulder.

"Tell me," she whispered.

When he was done, tears had bloomed in Silvestra's eyes. "It's so unfair," she said while he cradled her.

"I know," he said. "But I believe you. I know what you saw, what you felt, was real. I don't doubt it for a second."

Silvestra pulled back and stared at the man her heart now belonged to. He believed her. That simple statement did more for her ego, more for her senses than any declarations of love and promises.

Gingerly, Cal reached up and wiped one velvet tear as it fell down her cheek. "I love you, Silvestra. And because I do, I believe you, trust you. I love you. Let me show you."

His lips took hers with such tenderness and care, Shy felt herself floating on a cloud. The soft, needful moan that escaped from the back of her throat silently pleaded for more.

Their bodies embraced, locked together as Cal slid them to the floor in front of the fire, its warmth draping them. His mouth trailed a lazy line from her chin, down the long length of her neck to her shoulder, where his teeth pulled a thin strap of her nightgown from its resting place, revealing the perfect creamy flesh of her breasts to his view. With kneading hands, Cal cupped the swollen mounds together and made love to each of them with his tongue, his mouth, his breath.

Silvestra arched, the air hissing from her. When Cal took one hardened rosy nub in his mouth and sucked at it greedily, like a hungry baby, Silvestra lost all remnants of sanity. Blinding light and searing heat dissolved through her. Nothing had ever felt like this before. Felt this good, this unbelievably good. A lifetime spent keeping her emotions under control, never showing the turmoil, the needs, the wants that were inside, quivering to come out were now all forgotten, as Silvestra let herself feel free for the first time.

Clutching his hair, folding herself to him, Silvestra's hands snaked into his shirt, undid the buttons, and then flayed back the material so she could roam unopposed. A thin line of sweat fell from his collarbone, and she rose for a sample. He tasted tangy, exotic, cured with an inner spice and flavor that was as familiar to her now as her own name.

Cal tugged down the remainder of the nightgown. His tongue flicked down her flat stomach, stopping briefly at the scar, and then moving down to her thighs. Parting them with his nose, his mouth found that delicate, delicious nub that made her woman. When his lips closed over it, she cried out, then let the waves of pleasure roll through her.

All reason flew. All thoughts died. They became touching, feeling, pleasure beings, intent on one purpose and one purpose alone.

Cal tore at his clothes, throwing them off. His hands cupped the back of Silvestra's neck as he pulled her down fully to lie on the rug. His eyes were half-moons burning with a passion and desire that made her blood boil. When she opened for him, greedily taking all he was, some small portion of her knew the peace that a simple death could bring.

Moments later time stopped for them both.

Silvestra heard his heart pulsing. She lay with her head on his chest, their bodies wrapped in an intimate lover's embrace.

"It amazes me that at the ripe old age of thirty-five, this is the first time in my life I've ever really made love to a woman," Cal said.

Silvestra smiled and lifted her head. "You have a way with words, Sheriff."

Rubbing a finger down her bare arm, Cal sighed. "I guess it just took me a while to find the right woman."

Tears instantly sprang to Silvestra's eyes.

"I've told you before you have a rather frank way of putting things," she said.

"I mean it, Silvestra. You can't deny this is meant to be. Perfect."

She shook her head. "No. It is. I can feel it, too."

One bushy black eyebrow cocked upward. "Why do I feel there's a 'but' in there?"

She was silent a moment, trying to work it all through. "I've had so little in my life that has been. Giovanni, really, was the only thing I ever considered perfect."

"Tell me about him. I want to know."

Cal cradled her in his arms, resting his cheek against hers, and asked, "You had to have him by Caesarian, didn't you?"

"Yes. He was so big, over eight and a half pounds. I...I couldn't deliver him naturally. For a long time, I felt guilty about that."

"Rose had the girls by section. She used to say she didn't feel like a real mother, having them taken from her, not being able to deliver them herself."

"That's the way I felt. But, then I had my baby in my arms, knew I was his mother, so it didn't make a difference how he came into the world, just that he was safe and healthy and mine."

Nodding, Cal said, "That's what Rose said, too. "

"Smart woman, your sister."

"She is that. Tell me about your husband," Cal said, winding his fingers into her hair. "All I know is he was your therapist, and much older than you. Did you love him very much?"

She sighed and snuggled closer to him.

"Aside from my parents and the Adams'," Silvestra said, "Paul was the only person who believed me when I was a child. He accepted my gift, never questioned it, never made me feel foolish or strange. I began seeing him after I started having panic attacks. He helped me through them, taught me how to deal with them. When my parents saw how helpful he was, they insisted I continue with the therapy. I did until I was eighteen."

"Then what happened?"

She was quiet for a while and Cal let her be.

"I quit going when I entered college. By then I'd helped the police a few times and some families individually with locating missing children. I hadn't seen Paul in months when suddenly he showed up at school one day. I could tell he was nervous about something, but never dreamed what it was. We went out to lunch and he confessed that he'd fallen in love with me. He knew the twenty-three-year age difference might be a problem, but he told me he wanted to marry me.

"I was shocked. I'd never guessed at his feelings."

"What did you do?"

"I'd known him most of my life, felt more comfortable with him than most people my own age, and because he knew the innermost workings of my mind, I allowed myself to think I was in love with him too."

"Allowed yourself? You weren't sure?"

"Not really, no. I wanted to love him, I really did. He was so good to me, for me. Gentle and kind. I believed I was in love with him and we married."

Cal recalled the wedding photo he'd seen on the computer. Both of them had looked nervous, strained. He was beginning to know why.

"There was a lot of press about our wedding," she said as if reading his mind. "Most of it was negative, citing the age difference and my youth. But we were happy together. If I never fell in love with him, I did grow to love him. Can you understand the difference?"

"Yes, I think I can."

"He took care of me, trusted me, believed in me. Everything I'd ever hope for. Soon, we had Gio, and we were even happier. Our marriage wasn't perfect. None is. Compromise was hard for Paul. Plus, he was a worrier. Every time I had to go away he wanted to come, to make sure I was okay, not working too hard, not being stressed. The obligations of his practice and the need to take care of our son prevented him. Sometimes...sometimes I thought he'd grown to resent my...gift. Sometimes, I felt like he hated it."

She grew quiet again.

Cal's heart melted. Married to a man she was comfortable with, but didn't really love must have been difficult. And yet, she hadn't said it was, made it seem like all was well and good. She would, he thought. She was that kind of woman. Willing to sacrifice, willing to compromise. Willing to do what needed to be done to carry on. A woman filled with contradictions. Cool and composed on the outside, a cauldron of burning passions within. Instinctively, Cal knew that the man she'd called husband had never opened those passions, had never made them come forward. The first time they'd made love, Silvestra had confessed she'd never felt that kind of release before. Now, he knew why. A passionless marriage; and now, a passion-filled romance.

"He hadn't wanted me to go to New York. We had a huge argument about it before I left."

"But you did go."

"Yes. In the end, he relented, apologized for being selfish. That was Paul. He got all his feelings out then apologized for them. A typical therapist."

Because she did, Cal chuckled along with her. There was no malice in her tone, just bold understanding.

"Sometimes, after the accident, I would think about what would have happened if I'd listened to him, just that one time, and not gone where I was needed. I could see us with the new baby, all of us, happy, content."

Cal rubbed a hand up her arm. "You don't know that for sure, Silvestra."

She sighed. "No, I don't. And I've stopped berating myself for thinking it." She propped up on one elbow, stared down at him. "You've helped with that. You've made me see there's more to life than remembering the past, dwelling on the pain. You've made me feel again, Cal, when I never thought or hoped I would."

It wasn't a declaration of love, he thought, but close to it.

A small yawn bubbled up from within her. He lifted and carried her back to the bedroom; kissed her gently.

She cuddled close to him, savoring the warmth, the strength that flowed from him.

"Get some sleep," he said, kissing her brow. When she didn't respond, he knew she already was.

Screams tore him awake.

Cal shot bolt upright as if a fist struck him in the midsection. Next to him, Silvestra was sitting on her knees, her breathing rapid and shallow.

Pulling her to him, running hands down her hair, across her face, he said, "My God, Silvestra, you're shaking like a leaf. What happened?" He turned the bedside light on and was shocked by what he saw.

Her face was as pale as a shroud; ashen, like someone lost in shock. The small brown mole seemed black against the pallor. Trembling lips held a chalky caste. But it was her eyes that tore at Cal's heart. They were dull and desolate, bearing none of the sparkle he'd grown used to, depended on. Like a sleepwalker, they held no life.

"What's wrong?" he repeated. "Did you have a nightmare?"

Silvestra swallowed. Her entire body racked with quaking. Her skin was like ice against his. "No. Not a nightmare. I thought at first...but...it wasn't."

Cal squinted. "You had another vision."

She nodded. "I thought it was a dream but when I felt my hands and they were so cold, I knew it wasn't. I waited and it came, slowly at first, but then so fast I couldn't take it all in."

Cal heard the frenzy creeping into her rapid speech and tried to calm it away. Rubbing some warmth back to her limbs, he coaxed her on.

Silvestra pulled away from his embrace and faced him.

"I saw Pris Bolton, lying on her back. She was face up, her eyes white and wide with shock. There was so much blood, so much!" Dropping her head in her hands, the tears flew down her pale cheeks. "Oh, God, Cal! She was dead. Stone cold dead."

The hiss of air that escaped him echoed through the room.

He forced his brain to think. "Where?" he asked, already grabbing for his clothes.

"I don't know, I've never seen it before."

"Can you describe it?"

"I, I think so, I'm not sure. There was so much blood, around her face, around her neck, just dripping like a faucet -"

"*Stop it.*" His hard shake brought her back to earth.

"I'm sorry," she whispered through a sob.

Cal pulled her to him, breathed in the scent of her hair. If he allowed himself, he would be shaking as badly as Silvestra was.

"Try and concentrate," he said. "Tell me what the surroundings look like."

Silvestra closed her eyes and took a few deep breaths. When she opened them Cal had a sense she wasn't really looking at him. She was far away, seeing again what she'd been so recently forced to view.

When she spoke, her voice was small, yet he could hear the control, the command she'd forced into it.

"There's hay. Lots of it. I can smell it. Pris is lying on it."

He watched her eyes move back and forth.

"It's a barn. Not cows, though...horses...I can hear whinnying close by...there's something above her on the wall...there's blood on it...there's blood on everything."

The slight catch in her voice was quickly checked.

"It's a saddle, an unusual one. Italian leather...red and black...the buckles look like gold."

"That's Priscilla's saddle. She had it made special when she was in Europe two years ago. Can you see anything else, any other identifying sign?"

Silvestra peered straight ahead as she walked through the scene. "The walls are a strange color. Bright, strange."

Something sparked in him. "Orange? Like a tabby cat orange?"

"Yes! Do you know where it is?"

"Yeah." He finished dressing and was halfway to the door before she caught him.

"I'm going with you," she said, pulling back his arm.

The look in his eyes told her no.

"Please."

The plea knocked at his heart. "Get dressed," he said. "Quickly."

"Where are we going?" she asked, two minutes later, seat-belted in the squad.

"The Bolton ranch. The place you saw is the horse barn."

"Why is it that strange color?"

At any other time, and for any other reason, Cal might have laughed. The color had been in deference to Pris. She'd wanted it and fought her father long and hard to have the stalls painted the bright color. He remembered the first time he'd seen it.

Cal wasn't looking forward to seeing it again.

They were at the ranch in less than ten minutes.

The house was, as expected, dark. Cal cut the lights on the squad and drove around the property gate past the cattle barns to the horse stalls.

"Stay here," he told Silvestra as he got out of the car.

She was standing next to him less than a second later.

"You don't usually do as you're told, do you?" he asked, glancing down at her.

He was relieved to see the pallor gone. Amber eyes were once again bright, the gold flecks in the centers burning brightly.

"Not usually."

Cal pursed his lips. "Come on, then, and be quiet."

The door to the barn stood unlatched, the bolt lying haphazardly on the ground at their feet. A single light shone from somewhere in the interior of the building.

Cautiously, Cal slid the door open, Silvestra glued to his side.

Cal turned and motioned her to stay behind him. Together they entered.

The smell hit them like a brick in the face.

Silvestra covered her mouth and nose with her hands. Stealing himself, Cal went further into the barn. He knew where Pris kept her prized saddle.

The smell drew him to her. She was just as Silvestra had described. Lying flat on her back, eyes wide with shock, blood, congealed now from time, covering her torso and face. Cal looked around the body trying to find the weapon that had ravaged her so completely. He found nothing.

In death, Priscilla Bolton's beauty had been obliterated.

"We'd better call this in," Cal said, backing away. When Silvestra didn't follow, he glanced around. She was standing off to one side, leaning against a wall, staring down at the dead woman.

"Silvestra?"

She didn't respond.

Cal moved closer, grabbed her hand. It was frozen.

"His arms are branded," she said. Cal heard the drowsy tone and knew at once what was happening. Remaining silent, he let her go through the vision.

"They're strong...hard. He uses them for work. The muscles in his forearms are corded, twisted."

Her eyes were glistening, gleaming in the small light of the barn.

"They're arguing...her face is angry. She's shouting at him...something... She starts to leave, turns, doesn't see the knife...he pulls it out of a case from behind his back. He's used the knife before, knows what to do with it. He grabs her around the neck, pulling her off balance. I can't see his face, Pris's head is in front of it. He says something. Her eyes widen...she can't believe him...doesn't believe. He slices the knife across her throat, drops her to the floor...the blood comes in spurts, gagging her, drowning. He steps back to watch her die...he's breathing hard and fast..."

Silvestra's voice broke.

"He's excited by what he's done...his body reeks with elation...with life. *My God!*"

She pulled out of the vision and sank to the floor.

"Cal." Silvestra's eyes opened, focused.

"You scared the hell out of me," he said, dread dripping from his voice.

He'd lost his color, his lips were pale. A ring of sweat coated his upper lips and his brow was corrugated deeply from side to side.

"He's happy he killed her," Silvestra said, pushing against him to stand.

"Who? Who did this?"

Silvestra shook her head. "I couldn't see his face. I don't know."

"You said his arms were branded. Did you mean tattooed?"

Eyes squinting, she tried to remember. "No, not tattoos. I couldn't see it clearly. I'm sorry."

"You saw Priscilla murdered clear enough. My skin was crawling the whole time you were speaking. Is it always so vivid for you? So stark and coarse?"

Silvestra looked up at him, anxious to see his face. She was terrified of the derision she heard in his questions, panicked at the thought he'd find her freakish as so many others had.

But his feelings were clearly written in the concern she saw in his eyes. She cupped his cheek. "Yes. They are."

"*Dear Lord.*" With a savage thrust, he pulled her against him. Silvestra was stunned to feel his body shaking.

"I can't imagine how you stay so untouched by this," he whispered into her hair. "So normal."

If he'd told her he loved her and wanted to spend the rest of his life with her, Silvestra couldn't have been more thrilled than by those simple words.

Untouched.

Normal.

She'd been fighting her entire life for a sense of normalcy, for people to believe she wasn't odd, an aberration.

Cal's acceptance touched her more completely than Silvestra ever imagined it could.

In his strong, capable arms she felt content; at peace; whole again.

He gave her that and asked nothing in return.

"You'd better call this in," she said, repeating his words.

Chapter Ten

"She's been dead at least four hours." Doc Lynton stood from Priscilla's body. "Whoever did this was strong. She's cut clean to the spine and some of that's severed, too."

He snapped off his sterile gloves and threw them into a nearby garbage can. The aging doctor ran both hands through the thin white hair at his temples then bent back and forth.

"So probably killed around or before midnight?" Cal asked.

"Close to it. When I get her back to the office, I'll be able to do a more thorough examination." He latched his medical bag and stared directly at the Sheriff. His tired, old brown eyes were glowing with heat and anger. "You find out who did this, son. You find out fast. I brought that girl into the world. Whoever did this deserves to be taken out of it."

Cal nodded, his sentiments similar. He turned and saw Harv helping one of the county ambulance drivers place Priscilla's body into a black bag. The State Troopers had been called and Cal had a word with the Captain about the case. It was barely an hour since he'd walked up to the main house, woken Nate and Glory, and told them the horrible news. Glory, garbed in a flannel nightgown, hair done up in foam curlers, collapsed in her husband's arms. Nate, gray with shock, carried her to a nearby couch. Questions needed to be asked, but Cal didn't have the heart for it at that moment.

Knowing it was time, he walked slowly back to the house.

The entire ranch had woken. Cowboys, shirtless, garbed only in jeans and boots, stood around the kitchen, the hallway, murmuring to one another about how horrible it all was.

Cal made his way to the living room and found the family huddled together. Glory sat on the couch, sobbing, Nate's arm slung across her shoulders. Ethan stood by the unlit fireplace, his face tight and unreadable. He was fully dressed in a long-sleeved shirt, jeans, and boots.

Silvestra had been placed in the squad and told to stay there. Cal didn't want her to be part of this nightmare any more than she had to.

"Nate," Cal said, entering the room. "I need to ask you some questions."

The face that stared at the Sheriff seemed older than its fifty-five years. In the few short hours since they'd met at the police station, the rancher had aged a dozen years.

"Did Pris say she was going out tonight, maybe to meet someone?"

Nate glanced down at his wife, shook his head.

"When was the last time any of you saw her?"

Glory looked up and sighed. "It was about eleven, I think. I saw her light on, so I went into her room to say good night."

"Was she in bed?"

"No. She was standing by the window. Thinking, she told me."

"What about?"

Glory sighed again and wiped a tear. "Priscilla Ann never confided in me much, Sheriff. Tonight was no exception."

He nodded. "Had she been seeing anyone new lately?"

It was Ethan who replied. Turning from the fireplace, he regarded Cal with pure, raw loathing. The younger man's eyes flashed spite and flames. "No one since you crawled out of her bed for something better."

"Ethan." Both parents admonished.

"It's true, and you both know it. He used her and then dumped her like garbage. And just who had a fight with her tonight for all the town to see, huh? Him! Looked like he wanted to wring her neck. I don't think we have to look far for Pris's killer."

Cal checked the flash of temper that sparked through him. Ethan's words were as much from grief as from hatred. Turning to Nate, he said, "You know no matter what's happened between Pris and me in the past, I could never do something like this to her. To anyone."

Ravaged blue eyes glared back at him, tears lining their edges.

"Don't believe him, Pa," Ethan said, fists clenched at his sides. "You saw him. He was gonna grab Pris and slap her."

"Is that true, Cal?"

All eyes turned to the sound of the voice. One of the State Troopers had entered the room, unnoticed, Silvestra at his side.

"Is it?" he repeated.

"Yes," Cal said, jaw tight. Concisely, he told the trooper about the cattle and the meeting held earlier. "Priscilla was making accusations against..." Cal's eyes flicked to Shy and then back to Trooper White's. "Someone she had no cause to and I got angry. But I didn't kill her."

"Ask him where he was during the time Pris was killed," Ethan spat.

Just as Cal was about to answer he was stopped dead in his tracks by Silvestra's calm avowal. "With me. All evening, after the meeting."

Every eye in the room turned to her.

"Cal didn't kill, Pris, Trooper White. You have my word on that."

"Your word? " Ethan moved towards her in a flash.

Silvestra didn't flinch.

Lips curled back, eyes pinpoints, Ethan glared at her and said, "Who the hell are you? Nothing queer ever happened around here until you came to town. That was one thing Pris was right about tonight. The cattle deaths started with you when you supposedly found one of ours. How do we know you didn't kill it? How do we know you didn't kill any of them? Or my sister? I bet Pris would still be alive if it weren't for you."

Silvestra's eyes stayed level, hands folded in front of her. Her calm demeanor never wavered with the cruel words. Dismissing him and his rage, she turned to Ed White and introduced herself, adding, "I saw Pris killed in my mind. Vividly. I detailed everything to Sheriff Blackbear. From the description I gave, he was able to figure out where her body was. We arrived together and found her."

Ed squinted, rubbed a hand over his stubbly face. "Coeltrain?" he asked. "Like in S.G.Coeltrain?"

"Yes."

"Mac Granger is an old buddy of mine. We were in Kabul together. I've heard him mention your name more than once on our yearly fishing trips. Just put it together."

Silvestra managed a weak smile. "I've worked on a number of cases with Captain Granger."

"He's a good man," Ed said. "Good cop, too."

"You don't seriously believe any of this crap?" Ethan's gasp broke through the room like a hurricane. "They're probably in it together. Wanted to get Pris out of the way, I'll bet. You didn't like her, she told me herself."

"Mr. Bolton, I barely knew your sister. I met her two times and both of those times she made her disdain for me obvious to anyone who saw it. I chose to ignore it and her."

"*You bitch!*"

He was agile and quick as he pulled back a fist to strike her. Cal was quicker.

In one move the Sheriff stopped Ethan's hand from striking, doubled the arm around his back, and forced him, face down, to the floor.

"Get off me!" the younger man shouted, writhing beneath the deadly grip.

"Take it easy son," Ed said. "Let him up, Cal."

Reluctantly, the Sheriff pulled back. Ethan shot up like a bullet. "You're gonna regret that." White teeth were clenched, eyes on fire.

"That's twice in the course of a few hours you've threatened me," Cal said, the words slicing through the room like a saber. "I don't think you want to go for three."

Ethan drew back, snarling. "You son of a -"

"Stop it!" Glory shouted. "Stop it." Springing up to her son, one hand caught him squarely across the cheek. The look of revulsion on her face was distinct against the pallor and sorrow. "This isn't helping! I won't have you acting like a crazed animal, do you hear?"

Silvestra watched, amazed, at the turn in him. Ethan became almost sheepish under his mother's scorn, stooping his shoulders, his blond head hanging in shame.

The room stood quiet, the sound of a mother's slap still echoing through it. Glory turned her anger to Cal. "I don't believe you could have done this to Pris. But if I find out you did, you won't live long enough to regret it." She spoke with brutal determination and a grave neutrality, voice flat and deadly. Her green eyes grew hard and cold as blocks of ice when her gaze raked past him to Silvestra.

Glory yanked the belt on her robe firmly, then strode from the room, hands clenched so tight, Silvestra knew her palms would have fingernail indentations.

Ethan, head still lowered, followed her lead after throwing one last look of contempt at the Sheriff.

Tongue tucked in one cheek, Ed White regarded Cal, then Silvestra, and then the Sheriff again. Taking a deep breath, he said, "Cal, maybe under the circumstances it'd be better if you removed yourself from this case."

A muscle in the corner of Cal's eyes spasmed. "Now wait a minute, Ed." There was a hitch of controlled fury in his voice. "You can't think I had anything to do with this."

"Of course not," came the quick reply. "But you *are* personally involved. I think in the eyes of fairness it might be better if the Sheriff's office deferred this one to us and played second string. And face it, I have more manpower available than you do."

The room grew deathly silent, the air surging with hot choler. Shy watched Cal's face, imagining the debate going on inside him.

"Together," he said forcefully. "We work on this together. I won't have someone with a grudge against me make me run with my tail between my legs."

Silvestra told herself at that moment she'd never loved anyone more than Caleb Blackbear.

Ed waited before replying. "We'll track any lead, then, even if it leads, as young Bolton thinks, to you."

"Fine. Now let's get started."

As partners, both men began questioning the ranch hands and the household staff. After a brief conversation with Harv, Cal told Silvestra the deputy would drive her home. Since there was nothing more she could do, she agreed.

It was daybreak when she finally fell into bed, exhausted.

Fighting sleep, her mind went over everything she'd seen at the Bolton's. There was something, some little thing familiar in the flash she had of Pris' killer. What was it? Silvestra closed her eyes and willed the scene to return.

There was the killer's back, the line of the shoulders. The hair color was muted from the faint lighting in the barn. Light, though. Maybe red or dark blond.

She'd told Cal the arms were branded.

Branded?

What did it mean?

Branded.

Silvestra tried to sort the puzzle out, but her brain was too tired, too depleted to think logically.

Finally, the fatigue engulfed her.

Cal rubbed his eyes with the pads of his thumbs and fought back a yawn.

"Been a busy night," Harv said, placing a cup of fresh, hot coffee on the Sheriff's desk.

"You won't get any argument from me." He took a long, deep draught of the jet black fluid and sighed.

It was past nine a.m. After sending Silvestra home, Cal and Ed White had systematically searched the barn again for clues to Priscilla's killer, and more importantly, why she'd been killed. That done, the two lawmen went through the dead woman's room and belongings. They found nothing of any significance.

The state troopers sealed off the barn and the outlying property and were presently combing the area.

Cal picked up the phone before it finished its first announcing ring. "Blackbear. Yes...how big?" He searched the desk for a pencil, found one, and began writing. "Okay...thanks, Doc."

"Lynton?" Harv asked.

"He just finished with Pris. He thinks the knife that sliced her was along the lines of a Bowie or a big hunting blade. One that's used for gulleting. Thick plated because of the size and width of the slash across her neck."

Harv ran a hand through his hair and sighed. "Well, that makes every male in Renewal above the age of ten a suspect."

"Doc said her spinal cord had been severed at the base of the neck. So whoever did it wasn't too tall."

"How'd he figure that?"

"The slice was straight from side to side. Someone tall would have made a downward tear, someone shorter, upward. Silvestra told me the killer was speaking directly into Pris's ear when he was holding her from behind."

"So whoever did it is roughly five-eight or around that. That lets you out for sure."

Cal looked up at his deputy. The lopsided grin faded at the Sheriff's killer perusal.

"Sorry," he murmured. "Bad joke."

Something clicked in Cal's brain, forgotten until that moment. "Silvestra had a vision of the killer," he told Harv. "She mentioned branded arms. What does that sound like to you?"

"Tattoos?"

Cal shook his head. "She said no. Branded." He sat back and steepled his fingers. "I can't figure it out. If not a tattoo, what?"

"Scars?" Harv said. "Could it be scarring like, you know, from a burn or accident?"

Cal slowly nodded. "Maybe. Sounds plausible. I'll call Shy and put it to her."

Just as his hand went to the phone, it rang.

"Blackbear."

"Think I discovered what's been killing the cattle," Rand Denny said without preamble.

"Where are you?"

"Oklahoma City. I just got back the preliminary results on the serum samples I sent in on Ben's animals. It showed high concentrations of potassium chloride. I'm having one of the techs here run Amos' samples through quickly to see if we get the same results."

"What is it, a drug?"

"Not like you mean. We give potassium for a variety of reasons. I won't go into them now because they're complicated and boring, but the finding of it in the serum could be consistent with the physical findings of enlarged hearts. An overdose of it could lead to rapid heart failure and overload."

"Where can you get stuff like this? Can you buy it over the counter?"

"No. It's got to come straight from a doctor or a vet's supply, or a prescription from a pharmacist. You could order it from a drug company, I suppose, but I doubt it would be sold to a layman."

Cal thought for a moment. "You have this stuff at your place?"

"Tons of it."

"Would you know if any was missing?"

"Not unless I did a full-scale check of the inventory. My office manager might be able to help, though. Why? You think someone stole it from my clinic?"

"If, as you said, it can't be gotten any other way, either you or Doc Lynton are the most likely people in town to have it on hand. How soon are you coming back?"

"I should have the rest of the results within an hour. I can make it back before noon."

"Call me as soon as you get in."

Cal quickly replayed the conversation to his deputy. "You go over to Lynton's. Ask him to check his supply."

"Where're you headed?" Harv asked as Cal put on his hat then squarely yanked it in place.

"Denny's."

Five minutes later he arrived at the vet's clinic. After explaining the conversation he'd had with her boss, Cal requested Sarah Monroe check their inventory of the drug. She led him down the same corridor he'd taken the previous night.

"We keep everything in here," she said, opening the door to a room Cal hadn't noticed before. Inside were numerous metal shelves extending from the floor halfway up to the ceiling, filled with boxes and cartons. Each carton was wrapped with clear plastic, marked with the name of the drug and a label detailing what company it had been purchased from. There were hundreds of small bottles of clear and opaque fluids, boxed drugs, and even materials for intravenous setups and solutions.

"You look fairly well stocked."

Sarah smiled. "Rand believes in keeping lots of inventory on hand. Most of it doesn't expire for years. The stuff that does quicker, we just re-order more often." She bent to a file cabinet, opened it, and flipped through a few folders with her fingers.

"Here we go." She pulled out a sheet and gave it to him. "Those numbers on the right are the stock numbers, the left shows the amount taken, the date, and the remaining number of vials left. Either Rand or one of the techs sign them out. Let's check and see if this all corresponds."

Together, they worked, finding and cataloging each box of potassium chloride.

"That's strange," Sarah said, placing a finger across her lips. "What was that last number?"

"0073"

She rummaged through the shelf, then went to the next one. "I can't find it."

"Let me help."

They moved cartons from one shelf to another, looking for the errant box.

"I don't see it anywhere," She said.

Cal looked at the inventory sheet. "16 vials of it were left in the carton according to this."

"Yes." Her brow furrowed as she chewed her upper lip. "I can't explain it."

"No one is allowed back here?"

"No. Just Rand, the techs, and myself."

Cal looked at the sheet again. "The last time one was signed out for was over a month ago," he said. "I need to see a list of all the clients Denny's seen since then."

Sarah stared at him for a few seconds. "I don't know if I should do that, Sheriff. Client confidentiality and all."

His black eyes bore into hers. "Sarah, don't make me go get a warrant. It'll just waste valuable time."

Her eyebrows rose. "I guess I can let you look. Come on."

At the reception desk, Sarah flipped through the appointment book. "The names written in red are office visits. The ones in blue are farm visits. It makes billing easier."

Cal scanned the sheets, recognized all the names listed. "Rand's practice is pretty busy, isn't it?"

"Lately it seems like he's never here except at night."

Cal flipped a page and saw a name he hadn't expected. "Pris Bolton was in on the fifteenth."

Sarah scanned the listing. "Yes. She brought her mother's cat in for some complaint. I don't think Rand found anything wrong with it. Terrible business about her. Heard about it on the radio when I was coming in this morning. You trying to find out who killed her?"

Cal didn't answer. Instead, his mind went into overdrive. Pris had been in to see Denny eight days ago. Ben's cows had been discovered two days after that, Amos' yesterday. And now Pris was dead. "Did you talk to her about anything while she was here? Anything unusual?"

Sarah shrugged. "The weather, mostly. Pris isn't...wasn't the kind to make small talk with women."

"Did she ask you about any drugs, clinic procedures, or anything along those lines?"

Squinting, she replied, "No, why? Why would she ask me about stuff like that."

Cal ignored the question. "I need to take one of those vials of potassium with me. I need to show it to someone."

"I guess you could," she said. "You're not gonna tell me what this is all about, are you?"

"Police business," he said. "Rand knows about it, though, so don't worry."

A minute later he left the clinic, a full vial of potassium in his pocket. He sped out to the Bolton ranch and located Ed White, telling him about Rand's discovery and Pris's visit to the clinic.

"You think they may be linked?" the trooper asked.

Cal shrugged. "I don't know. But this is what Denny thinks has been killing the animals." He pulled the bottle from his pocket. "Show it to your men and have them keep their eyes open. I'm going to talk with Nate and Glory."

Up at the house, Cal heard shouting when he entered the foyer.

"Well, where the hell is he?" Nate bellowed. "He didn't say anything to you about where he was going?"

"I already told you," Glory answered. Cal could hear the tears and frustration in her sobs. "He never said a word to me. I just caught him going out. He never answered me when I called out to him."

"That boy's been acting strange lately. He's never home, won't talk to me. Something's not right. I'm worried he's using -"

"Excuse me," Cal said from the doorway. He wasn't pleased when Glory stiffened at the sight of him. "I need to talk to you both."

"Haven't we been bothered enough for one day?" Glory asked, lips curving downward.

Cal removed his hat and advanced into the room. "I'm sorry. I know how difficult this is for you both."

"Do you?" Her tone dripped with venom.

"Hush, woman," Nate admonished with a scowl. She glared at her husband, fixed Cal a level stare, and then strode from the room.

Nate visibly shrank with his wife gone. The older man crossed to the bar and poured a glass of scotch. Despite the hour, he drained most of it in a single gulp. "I'm sorry about Glory. She's not herself. None of us are today. This business with Pris, well, it's been more than she can handle. They were never close, those two, fought like coons and bears most days. But she was our daughter." He stopped, drained the glass, and poured another. "And now this business with Ethan. That's upset her even more."

"What's happened to him?"

Nate swirled the liquid in his glass. "Seems he's gone off somewhere without telling anyone where he was headed. Been doing that more and more lately. Frankly," his weary eyes found Cal's. "Frankly, I've been worried he's into something bad."

"Such as?"

Nate took a deep breath and then a drink. "Drugs. He had a problem with them as a teen. You might not remember. Seems I recollect you were away at college at the time. We sent him away for treatment after the accident."

Cal's black eyes narrowed. "What accident?"

"Wrecked one of the jeeps. He was high as a kite, took it out for a joyride, and wound it around the side of the barn. Was in the hospital for over two months with burns. Lately, I've noticed he's been acting strange, distant, moody again like before."

Cal's mind clicked. "Nate, what kind of drugs did he do?"

Refilling his glass for the third time, he downed half of it before replying. "Heroin. Injected it."

"I need to ask you to allow us to search Ethan's room. It may help discover why Pris was murdered."

And by whom, he silently added.

"Why?"

Cal related the findings Denny had discovered.

"You don't think Ethan had anything to do with this?" Nate boomed. "You can't. He isn't capable of something like that."

"Nate, I swear, I hope I'm wrong. But please, let us search his belongings."

Both men stared at one another, each convinced the other was wrong. Just as he was about to answer, Cayla, the Bolton's housekeeper, came in and told Cal there was an important call from Mrs. Coeltrain. He rushed to the nearest phone.

"Silvestra?"

"Thank God I finally found you."

He heard the desperation in her voice, could mentally see the anguish written across the face he'd come to know so well, to love so deeply.

"What is it?"

"I figured something out about Priscilla's killer. The branding marks I saw on the arms were old sc—"

The line went dead.

"Silvestra? Silvestra!" Cal's voice was steeped with fear.

He slammed the phone down and turned to Nate. "You said Ethan was treated for burns after the accident. Where were they?"

"His chest and arms mostly. Luckily, one of my hands pulled him out of the jeep before more damage could be done."

Cal bolted from the room before the rancher finished his sentence.

Chapter Eleven

Slowly, tortuously, Silvestra came back from the depths of unconsciousness.

A headache the size of a basketball made focusing hard. Something rough and coarse was wound around her mouth so tightly, the skin tingled from the restraint. Lying in a fetal position, her hands were bound from behind, attached in such a way that every time her legs moved, her arms were yanked backward, the rope holding them together cutting into her flesh.

Silvestra twisted side to side, trying to loosen the bond, but couldn't.

"Won't do you no good," a voice said from behind her. "I tied 'em the same way I do up a calf. You can struggle all you want, you won't get out of it."

The voice moved closer until Ethan Bolton stood above her, a lopsided, crazed grin on his face. "I think that's kinda fittin'," he said, squatting next to her. "Since you were so nosy about them dead cattle."

A maniacal cackle stopped Silvestra's heart cold.

He peered down at her, eyes narrowing to slits. "If it hadn't'a been for you telling Amos his worthless cows had been killed, we could have avoided all this."

He stood and moved to a window.

They were in a cabin sparsely furnished with a table, two wooden chairs and a set of bunk beds across one wall. Ethan had dumped her bound body on the floor in the center of the room.

She tried to struggle out of the bonds again but gave up quickly as the twine gashed through her skin. Staring at Ethan's back as he surveyed something out the window, she tried to think of something, *anything* that could help her out of this situation.

When she moaned, Ethan turned around.

Brows furrowed, his eyes bore into hers with such heated intensity, for a moment, Silvestra found her courage floundering.

"What's the matter?"

Raising her eyebrows, Shy shook her head from side to side to try and convey what she wanted. As loudly as she could, she moaned again.

"Christ woman, what is it?" He ripped the bandanna from her face in one jerky motion, causing her head to snap back and bang on the wooden floor. For a few seconds, dazed from the impact, she lay motionless.

"Please," she finally said, her voice dry and hoarse. "Please, Ethan, don't do this."

His blond head snapped back at the sound of her voice. "Pris said the same thing," he said softly, his eyes raking up and down her face. "Right before I killed her."

"Why?" Silvestra rubbed her tongue over parched lips and found no solace from their arid state. "Why did you kill your sister?"

"It's your fault," he barked, pointing an accusatory finger. "Everything was going exactly as we planned until you started up with your psychic babble. It spooked Pris. She wanted to stop. Thought we were gonna get caught, thought *you* were gonna finger us to Blackbear." His lips curled back at the name.

"Ethan, what are you talking about? I don't know anything about what you and Priscilla have..." The rest of the sentence died as she realized it all. That sudden charge when she'd first shaken hands with Pris had been a precursor, a forerunner of the trouble to follow. Up until now, Shy hadn't been able to understand the meaning of the cattle deaths, of why she'd seen visions of them. Now it was clear. Pris Bolton had been the link, the connection.

"Now, you don't expect me to believe you, do you? Pris told me herself when you shook hands she felt like someone shot a spark clean through her, like when she plugged in the hairdryer once with a wet hand. Spooked her royally. But she didn't know at the time you could do things with your mind, see things and all, until the meetin' last night. She got all panicky thinking we was gonna get found out."

Silvestra tried to sit up. The twine broke through her skin and she bit her lip to keep from crying out. She refused to let Ethan see the pain, the fear, knowing it would only feed his deranged ego. "I don't understand. Why did you kill those animals?"

"Well, now, that's kinda funny, too, you should ask." He stood, stretched, and smiled again. Silvestra checked the shudder that ran down her spine as he glared at her. "Since it was you who first put the idea in my head."

"What are you talking about?"

"You were the one who found our cow by the creek."

"So?"

"Well, after that I got this great idea. Pa is always bragging how our ranch is the number one producer in Renewal and for a hundred miles in all directions. Well, I wanted to make sure it was gonna stay that way since the ranch comes to me when the old man kicks. And from his latest checkup, that may be pretty darn soon."

Silvestra's arms and legs burned. She could no longer deny the agony her limbs were being put through. "Ethan, please," she said. "Please cut the connecting string. I promise, I won't try anything, I won't try to get away."

His casual shrug terrified her. "Wouldn't matter if you did. I can run faster than anyone I know. You'd never even get to the door."

From the side of his boot, he raised a small knife. With one brisk flick, the cord connecting her hands to her feet was split. Immediately Silvestra's arms recoiled at being set free and she cried out.

"Pain'll go away in a few minutes," he said, nonchalantly.

Scraping one of the chairs across the room, he yanked her from the floor by the upper arm. "Now, like I was telling you, I got this idea to make certain our ranch stayed number one."

Silvestra's vision clouded when Ethan roughly threw her into the chair. It was starting to settle again as she asked, "How?"

Keep him talking. Keep him focused on himself, not me.

Diverting his attention to himself and away from her would buy time. Time for Cal to find her.

Cal.

As Ethan droned on about a drug he'd read about in a farming magazine, Silvestra brought Cal's face to mind. Centering on him, his strength, his composure during times of stress helped keep the fear from taking over. While Ethan ranted about how Pris had stolen the drug from an unsuspecting Rand Denny, Silvestra remembered what it felt like to be held in Cal's strong and protective arms; how the sound of their hearts beating meshed so perfectly; how their lives, in so many ways, paralleled one another's. They were meant to find each other. All the tragedy of both their pasts had led them to this.

"It was a perfect plan," Ethan said, chest swelling. "Everything was going along just fine until you butted in. Now, I've got to get rid of you, too."

Silvestra's eyes widened as he stood and slowly pulled a long, thick-bladed knife from a bag slung across one of the bunks. A surge of energy emanated from the steel blade across the room and Silvestra instantly knew where the knife had been last.

Ethan swaggered towards her, a deranged smile crossing his face again.

"But first," he sneered, "We're gonna have us some fun, you and me."

The front door stood open and Cal pulled back. Drawing his revolver, he silently motioned for Ed and Harv to circle around towards the back of the cottage.

A thin trickle of fear beaded its way down his neck. Something was wrong. Something was missing.

Solomon.

The dog wasn't barking as he usually did whenever someone came to the door.

Standing level against the jamb, Cal shoved the door inward and flattened himself against the wood. After a few seconds, he peered, cautiously, inside. Seeing nothing unusual, with care, he made his way in. The phone sat, uncradled on the floor next to the loveseat. The monotonous dial tone echoed eerily in the room.

Cal walked from the living room to the kitchen and as he was heading towards the back, Harv burst in through the side door.

"Dog's out back," he said, breathless. "There's a big hunk of half-eaten meat by his side."

"Is he alive?"

"Barely. Ed went up to the house to get Jake. You find anything?"

"Not yet."

The house gave no clue as to where its occupant was.

"I know Ethan took her." Cal punched a fist into the wall. "Where? Where would he bring her?"

"Someplace where he thinks it's safe."

Cal's eyes found the picture on the mantel. He stared at Silvestra's image as anger and frustration seared within him.

"Cal!" Mabel and Jake rushed into the house. "What's happened?"

He told them. "Did you hear a car or truck drive up at all today?"

"No," Jake answered, throwing a comforting arm around his weeping wife. "We've been home all day, too."

"He's either on foot then, or took a horse," the Sheriff said. He bolted from the kitchen and began inspecting the yard. Eyes keenly focused, almost immediately he found the tracks.

"He's on horseback," he told the group, coming back into the house. "I'm driving to the Bolton's to get one. You coming?"

Deputy and Trooper nodded.

"I'll be back before you know it." He stepped toward Mabel, squeezed her upper arms. "I'll find her. I promise you."

The older woman regarded him through teary eyes. "I know you will."

Her conviction gave his feet wings.

Twenty minutes later, Cal, Harv and Ed rode back into the yard. "Follow them," Cal ordered, pointing to the tracks.

Chapter Twelve

"Ethan stop. Think about what you're doing, what you've done. This is wrong."

"*Shut up.*" Roughly, Ethan shoved her back down to the floor where she landed in a heap. Pain knifed through her spinal column, but Silvestra refused to cry out, to let her captor see her weak, knowing the madman would take full advantage of whatever frailty she showed.

"You talk too damn much."

When he laid the knife on the table and moved to her, a lurid gleam in his eyes, Silvestra tried another tactic. "Cal knows where I am," she said firmly. "He's on his way here right now."

Ethan's laugh echoed through the rafters. "Do you think I'm an idiot, woman? That trick is as old as the hills."

"It's true. I had a vision, days ago, of him here, rescuing me."

His eyes narrowed, lips curled. "If that's so," he said slowly, "Why didn't you tell him I was gonna bring you here? If he knows, he would'a done something to protect you, to stop me."

The twisted logic didn't deter her. "At the time I didn't know it was you; I couldn't see your face. I only saw Cal saving me, coming here and bringing me home."

Silvestra watched him work through her words. "It's the truth," she said, omitting the rest of the vision, the parts she'd been trying to erase from her mind.

Shy'd seen Cal with a knife identical to the one Ethan placed on the table, protruding from his shoulder. The day the vision came she'd been terrified. Now she couldn't breathe from the fear.

Ethan's left eye twitched at the corner as he ran a hand over the stubble on his chin. "I don't know whether to believe you or not."

Silvestra tried to keep her eyes level, steady. For the briefest of seconds, something flashed at the windows behind Ethan. It was gone so quick, she thought she'd imagined it.

"Nobody knows about this cabin 'cept my parents and a few of the hands," Ethan said, crossing his arms. "So I don't think your precious Sheriff will find us here. I think you're lying."

He moved stealthily towards her, striding with confidence. Taking up the knife, he ran a finger down the length of the blade. "But, if he does ever happen to find you, you won't look anything like you do now."

The feral grin stopped Silvestra's blood cold. With each small advancing step he took, she felt herself die a little.

"Now, about that fun I promised ya."

With the knife securely in his hand, Ethan knelt down on one leg and settled on top of her.

His body was so heavy, so solid, the air was pushed from her lungs when he covered her. Hot, fetid breath twisted down her neck and collarbone. Turning her face away, Silvestra tried to squirm, but to no avail. With hands still bound behind her, her shoulders had no leverage.

Ethan's mouth came up to her hair. "Pity to waste this," he said, "But you deserve it for interfering -"

The door flew open and in a flash of light, Silvestra saw Cal, Ed and Harv explode into the room. Like a firecracker, Ethan popped up and crouched, knife poised.

"Seems you weren't lying after all."

"Drop the knife, Ethan. You've got three guns pointed at your head."

Silvestra heard the measured steel in the Sheriff's voice.

"You don't scare me, Blackbear. If you were a real man and not some low-life half-breed, you'd take me hand-to-hand and not hide behind a weapon."

Silvestra watched the man she loved, saw the almost imperceptible tightening of his jaw. "No, Cal! Don't listen to him," she cried. "He's trying to goad you. Don't listen."

Ethan's lips pulled back in a snarl. "Don't listen, Cal," he mimicked. "She's already made a eunuch of you, Blackbear, like your mother did your father."

A low, deep, savage growl rumbled up from within Cal. Harv and Ed both instinctively closed ranks around him. "Cal, don't let him do this to you," Harv said. "He's worthless. You know it. We all know it."

The Sheriff ignored him, tossed his pistol aside, and said, "You want to prove you're a man, go ahead. I'm game."

"No!" Silvestra's eyes grew wide as saucers. This, *this* was the full extent of her vision. Combat between Cal and another man. She'd seen the outcome in her mind, dreaded it.

He disregarded her plea, crouching, ready to do battle.

Moving like the wind, Ethan advanced. His grip clutched at Cal's neck, pushing him backward.

Cal took the blow and yielded, pulling Ethan with him, knocking him off balance. With one flick of his wrist, Cal sent the younger man sprawling to the floor.

"Want more?" Cal asked.

Ethan grunted and shot up. Again, they grappled, hand to hand, legs twining, arms flying. Cal delivered two solid punches to Ethan's face. He retaliated by kicking the Sheriff once in the midsection. On the floor again, they rolled, pushed, kicked.

Horror washed over Silvestra, turning her insides to liquid.

Cal's knee landed squarely in Ethan's groin, causing the younger man to recoil and roll backward. Silvestra knew what would happen next. Before she could send Cal a warning, though, Ethan recovered and rolled back, the Bowie in his hands.

"Cal!" It was Ed's voice that boomed through the small room.

The Sheriff jumped up, hunched down in a fighting stance, but as quick as he was, Ethan was quicker. With a flick of his wrist, he landed the knife firmly in Cal's shoulder. He fell to his knees, one hand gripping the knife handle.

Ethan wasn't finished. With murder in his eyes, he sprang up.

The windows suddenly shattered as a million shards of glass blasted through the air.

In slow, suspended motion, Ethan flailed backward and fell to the floor, face-up, dead from the bullet to his forehead. Behind him, standing in the doorway, a shotgun still smoking, was his father.

"Cal!" Silvestra struggled against her bindings. "Cal!"

"I'm okay," he said. She could hear the life leaving his voice.

Trooper White walked guardedly to the doorway. "I'll take that now, Mr. Bolton," he said, voice calm and steady.

Like a man in a trance, Nate stared at the trooper, down to his outstretched hand, and finally to the shotgun. His face was a gray cloud, eyes devoid of life. Silently, he handed it over. Arms empty, he came into the cabin and knelt down next to his son.

"It's over, boy," Nate said. "It's over."

"Get me out of these things," Silvestra screamed. Ed took a small pocketknife from his pocket and tore through the bindings.

Once free, Silvestra sprinted to Cal's side. She hadn't realized she was crying until she saw the tears dripping down his face as she cradled it in her hands. "I knew you'd come," she sobbed.

Cal tried to smile, caressed her cheek with his free hand. "You okay?"

She nodded. "You need a doctor." She stared at the hole the knife had slashed in his shirt as the blood seeped from his arm.

"Silvestra," he murmured.

"Shush."

"I want to tell you something." He ran his tongue over his swollen lips. His breathing changed, slowed a bit. Silvestra knew the pain must be excruciating and yet he still fought it.

"They'll be plenty of time for talking after you see Doc Lynton. Save your strength for now."

"Shy, when I saw him on top of you -"

"Cal, stop. It's over."

He nodded, closing his eyes. "All I thought about was you, about him...hurting you."

"He didn't."

"Thank God."

Her eyes traveled to where father and son were huddled together. Nate's tears dropped freely, heart-wrenchingly, down his face while he held his son's head in his lap as he rocked back and forth. Silvestra couldn't begin to imagine the anguish Nate was going through, killing his only son.

She closed her eyes, took a deep breath, and then looked down into Cal's face once again. Silvestra watched as his eyes closed, knowing his hold on consciousness was slim.

Before succumbing to the inevitable, Cal looked up at her and whispered, "I love you."

Chapter Thirteen

Silvestra wiped away a tear and zipped up the garment bag.

Moving like a sleepwalker, arms, and legs heavy, she opened the armoire and began pulling out the rest of her clothes. Packing had never been one of her favorite things. Today, she hated it.

"What are you doing?"

She spun around as the sound of the voice sliced through the quiet room.

"Cal. I...I didn't know...you were...you're out of the hospital."

His black eyes watched her nervously as she wrung her hands together then took in the suitcases strewn about the room.

It had been one week; seven days since the incident at the Bolton cabin.

Ethan Bolton's knife had caused more damage to the Sheriff's shoulder than anyone had first thought. After an examination by Doc Lynton, Cal had been airlifted to the medical center in Oklahoma City and undergone five hours of surgery to repair the tears to the muscles and tendons that had resulted from the wound.

Silvestra had sat stonily silent in the waiting room, as if in a trace. She hadn't spoken to anyone, had refused all offers of food, conversation, and comforting.

Right now he looked so weak, standing there in faded jeans, a sling harnessing his left arm. Silvestra could see the cast encasing the limb went all the way across his chest, from front to back. She remembered what it had been like in the hospital, waiting for news of Cal's surgery. The doctors weren't sure he would ever have use of the arm again due to muscle damage. They weren't even sure he would survive the surgery due to the massive blood loss that resulted before treatment was started.

Silvestra's mind shattered. She couldn't lose him, too. She'd lost her other two reasons for living, she couldn't lose Cal as well.

But what if she did? What if he did die? How would she go on? Could she?

Did she want to?

Silvestra's mind and heart melded. She knew she wasn't strong enough to survive another loss of that magnitude. Fear scissored through her, cutting her insides to shreds.

When the doctors brought the good news Cal was fine, would probably have most of the use of the arm returned, Silvestra had already decided to run away. She couldn't shoulder the burden of loving someone so totally again. There was too much hurt involved, too much potential for pain. It was selfish, yes. She acknowledged that. But she had to go. She knew now any feelings of love she had would always be tainted, always be held up to standards that couldn't be met. Loving meant pain and heartache for her. Loving meant loss.

And now, she saw pain in Cal's eyes, across his frail face, and knew she'd caused it.

"I'm leaving in the morning," she told him, turning away to hide her tears.

"Where are you going?"

"Back to Boston. I have to start a book tour next week."

"You're leaving?"

"Yes."

"Just like that?"

She nodded.

When he spun her around Silvestra saw the pain had vanished, replaced by a blazing fury. He squeezed her arm, making her wince.

"No, Silvestra."

Brow furrowed, she said, "What?"

"No, you're not leaving. You're running away. I want to know why."

"I'm not running anywhere," she said, trying hard to control the shaking moving through her body. "I told you, I have a book tour next week. I have to go home and get ready."

"What about us?"

She didn't respond. Couldn't.

Releasing her arm, Cal stepped back. "Why weren't you at the hospital when I woke up?"

She shook her head, unable to answer.

"Do you know how crazy I was when you weren't there? I wanted to run out of that room, pull out all the lines and junk going into me and come here, find you, find out why you weren't there. It killed me Silvestra, do you understand that?"

She couldn't fight the tears any longer. Like a waterfall, they fell. She lifted her eyes to his, saw all the anger, the pain, the heartache housed in them.

Cal took one of her hands. "Why? Just tell me why? I thought...I thought we meant something to one another. I thought you might love me."

The misery was too much to hear in his voice.

"Can you possibly understand how scared I was?" she asked, her voice shaking. "The doctors said you might not live. They said it more than once until I finally believed them. Do you know what *that* did to *me*? To know I might lose you after we'd just found one another? All the feelings I had when Paul and Gio died came back. The fear, the guilt. God, the guilt!"

"You had nothing to do with what happened."

"I could have prevented it."

"How?" he asked. "You didn't know what was going to happen."

Silvestra took a deep breath, disgusted with herself for losing control. "Do you remember that day by the creek when I had a vision?"

He nodded. "You said it was personal, that you didn't want to talk about it."

"It was of you. I saw *you,* fighting with someone. I didn't know it was Ethan. I saw you take the knife in your shoulder. Don't you understand, Cal? I saw this happen to you and could have prevented it and didn't. Do you know how I feel about that?"

"You can't possibly blame yourself for this, Silvestra," he said quietly. "You said you couldn't see who I was fighting with. It might have been anyone, for any reason. A barroom brawl I had to break up, something else. Feeling guilty for what happened in that cabin is wrong."

Silvestra's voice broke into a thousand pieces of glass as she whirled on him. "Don't you dare tell me what I felt was wrong! You have no idea what I went through, seeing you...bleeding almost to death. Knowing I could lose you, and knowing I could have prevented it. You have no right to say what I feel is wrong. No right at all."

They stood rooted, staring at one another.

It was Cal who finally broke the silence. "I think it's more than that, Silvestra. Much more than feelings of guilt and remorse making you run away. I know you love me. I've never heard you say it, though I've dreamt you would. But I feel it. In all honesty, I think you're afraid."

Because the words hit too close to home for comfort, Silvestra turned from him, arms wrapped across her chest, as she walked to the window.

"You *are* afraid," he said. He came to her, turned around to face him again with his good arm. "Why?"

How could she tell him? It wouldn't make any sense to him; it barely did to her.

"Tell me, Silvestra. I have the right to know."

She raked trembling hands through her hair and sighed. "I'm not strong enough to love you, Cal. I realized that in the hospital."

"What do you mean, not strong enough?"

Her deep, bone-weary sigh was filled with all the misery, grief, and heartache she'd fed herself for the past week. "The thought you would die, that I would never have you in my life again, was too much."

"But I'm here. I'm fine."

"Yes, and thank God you are." Silvestra ran her hands up her arms to warm them. "I know you deserve an explanation, it's just so hard."

"I'm not going anywhere."

She gathered her thoughts, tried to make them sound coherent. "When Paul and Gio died, I thought I'd never be able to feel any kind of love again. It hurt so much, loving someone and then losing them. I didn't want that kind of hurt in my life again." She stared up into his face, lost in the blackness of his eyes. "But then I met you. I tried resisting it at first, these feelings running through me. But you were so persistent, so doggedly persistent. After a time, I thought I might be able to take the chance to love again. That I wouldn't feel the loss, the grief, anymore. In the hospital, I realized it's so easy to lose what you love. In a heartbeat, you could be gone, and I would be left again with nothing but a broken heart and spirit. I can't go through that again, Cal."

His brow pulled together. "You're saying you won't allow yourself to love me? Is that it? Because something may happen to me?"

"It's more, but yes, that's the way I feel. You're right, I am afraid."

"Silvestra, listen to yourself. There are no guarantees in life, no absolutes. I won't stand here and tell you nothing is ever going to happen to one of us, because it's not true. We could get sick, or hit by a car, or anything. To deny yourself the chance of being happy because you're afraid of something bad happening is juvenile. It doesn't make any sense."

"It does to me. And I know I'm not strong enough to go through it again."

"Yes you are, but you refuse to realize it. Look at all you've been through in your life, all you've suffered through, triumphed over. But you won't see all that. Instead, you want to hide behind a cold wall where nothing will touch you, nothing will invade your heart or your soul. You won't take a chance on loving me so you'll run away. Never mind what I feel, what I think."

"I don't expect you to understand. I'm sorry you feel that way."

"No, you're not. You wouldn't go if you were."

Cal began pacing around the room.

"All my life I've shut my heart away, thinking no one could ever really love me for who I am, what I am. I denied myself the pleasure of falling in love, not because I didn't want to be hurt. That was some of it, but really because I never truly felt good enough. I've been cheated out of happiness too many times by my own stupidity. Then you came into my life and accepted everything I was without question, without censure. I couldn't cheat myself this time, I knew what I felt for you was right, was good, was meant to be. I opened my heart, took a chance, and fell in love with you. I want a life with you, a long life, filled with children, with happiness, and even with some pain and heartache thrown in. That's normal. That's what life is about. I do a job where I can get hurt, yes. But in the three years I've held this office, this is the first time anything physical has ever happened to me. And because of it, you're willing to throw away a future that could be filled with love and satisfaction, just because something might happen. Because you may get hurt. You're right. I don't understand that, I never will."

Silvestra's face was ravaged by tears. Everything Cal said was true. She was afraid. Pure and simple.

"I have to finish packing," she said with a sniff. "Jake is driving me to the airport in Oklahoma City tonight. My flight leaves first thing in the morning."

Cal put his unbound hand in his pants pocket. She watched as he squared his shoulders, tired to school his features. But she could read the hurt in his eyes.

"I realize I've only known you for a short time, Silvestra, but from everything I've seen of you, from everything I've read about your past, I would never have pegged you for a coward."

With that, he turned and walked out the door.

Chapter Fourteen

Hundreds of eager faces, waiting in a gaggle of expectation, giggling, shouting, comparing favorite books, met Silvestra when she alighted from the limousine. An excited twitter started when one of the teenage girls spotted her, and before Silvestra got into the bookstore, the cheers became deafening.

"Goodness," Tracy Commons, her longtime agent said, hustling the both of them into the store. "This is the biggest crowd yet. Your hand is sure to be cramping by this afternoon."

Shy smiled, her eyes flowing over the sea of earnest faces. Thankfully, this was the last book signing on her three-week tour of the New England States. Tracy had arranged it so she finished up in Boston.

While Tracy introduced Shy to the bookstore manager, her mind deviated and rambled from the greeting.

One month today, she told herself. It's been exactly one month since I've seen Cal, since I left Renewal.

After embracing a tearful Jake and Mabel, Shy boarded the plane, hiding her swollen eyes behind large, thick sunglasses, and tried to ignore the searing pain jaunting through her system.

She was right to leave. It was the only fair thing for both she and Cal. What kind of relationship would they have had if all she did was continually worry something was going to happen to destroy it?

No, I was right to leave.

But why do I wake up in the middle of the night crying, calling out his name? Why can't I write, or keep any food down? Why won't this tormenting ache inside my chest go away?

Silvestra knew the answer but refused to accept it.

Instead, she'd thrown herself wholeheartedly into the book tour. She'd dragged Tracy with her all over New England, not wanting to be alone for a moment. When she was alone the pain grew worse. So, she'd persuaded her amiable agent to come along with her on every stop, every state. All of the book signings had been successful, Silvestra sometimes having to stay over the allotted time to accommodate every girl who'd been waiting.

She'd had her picture taken thousands of times by thankful mothers, as youthful arms with braces on their smiles draped around her, thrilled at having a photo with their favorite author.

"Well, let's get started." Tracy led Silvestra to the spot the manager had set up for the signing. The line jutted down the block from inside the bookstore.

Silvestra took her seat and smiled at her first fan of the day.

Silvestra handed the signed book back to the pudgy, bespectacled girl in front of her, with a smile.

When she turned to the next in line her eyes went wide.

"Winter? Summer?"

"Hi, Mrs. Coeltrain," the twins said together.

"How?...What are you girls doing here?"

"We're on break from school," Summer explained.

With a broad grin, her sister added, "And since he was coming out this way, Uncle Cal asked if we'd like to come along. To keep him company, you know?"

"Unc--"

Silvestra quickly turned, furtively searching everywhere. Her heart stopped when she found black eyes staring at her. All breathing ceased when he stepped from behind a book rack. And when he was standing in front of her, as his two nieces were, looking as handsome and wickedly attractive as always, Silvestra's mind stopped functioning.

"What are you doing here?" she asked, mouth as dry as a desert at noon, lips equally as parched.

"Silvestra, is something wrong?" Tracy asked.

"No, no, everything's fine Tracy. These are some...friends of mine." Her eyes hadn't left Cal's face for a second.

"We're from Oklahoma," Winter said, clutching the book Silvestra had yet to sign in her hands.

Remembering her manners, Shy made the introductions all around, her gaze habitually turning back to Cal.

Brows tight in thought, Tracy assessed the situation and addressed the girls. "Would you two like something to drink, or eat? The book store has a cafe upstairs."

"Cool!" Winter said.

"Can we, Uncle Cal?" Summer asked.

"Sure, go ahead. I'll be waiting here for you. Silvestra and I have a few things to discuss."

She couldn't breathe, didn't know if she could remember how. Like a starving woman, her eyes raked up and down his body, across his face, hungrily. In all the time she'd known him, Silvestra had never seen the Sheriff in anything other than his uniform or jeans. Now, he was wearing a tailored shirt with a sports jacket, pants, perfectly creased, with a bright tie. The one familiar thing about his attire were the boots, polished to a spit shine, on his feet, peeking out from beneath the hem of his pants.

She flicked her tongue across dry lips and inwardly groaned.

Why did he have to look so...amazing?

"Your arm is better," she said, noticing it was no longer in a cast.

"Docs in O.C. took the cast off three days ago. I can go back to work full time in a week."

"That's good news. I'm glad for you."

He nodded.

"What are you doing here, Cal?" she repeated.

His shrug was tense. "Like the girls said, we're on vacation. They always wanted to see the east coast, and since I was coming out this way anyway, I thought I'd bring them along."

"Why?"

"Why what?" His bushy eyebrows rose a fraction.

"Why were you coming east? What's here for you?"

His hard stare made her legs turn to jelly and Silvestra was happy she was sitting down or would have slithered to the floor. "You know the answer to that, Shy."

She swallowed the golf ball in her throat. "Cal, we were over all of this before I left. I thought-"

"Whatever you thought, Silvestra Coeltrain," he said, voice low as he bent down to eye level with her, "you thought wrong. Oh, I know what you told me before running away. I remember every word of that conversation. Tell me," he bent one knee, sliding his foot on her chair rung, making an escape impossible and bringing his head down closer. Silvestra could smell his cologne, could count the hairs at his temple. "Have you been sleeping well?"

Hypnotized, she said, "No."

He nodded. "Been worrying? Feeling fretful, teary?"

Silvestra swallowed again, "Yes."

Still nodding, he continued. "How 'bout a nagging, burning pain, oh, right about here." He pointed to the left side of his chest.

Tears started welling in Silvestra's eyes. Unable to speak, she took a cue from him and nodded.

"I thought so. Well, Silvestra, I'm not a doctor," he said, theatrically. "Don't even play one on tv. But I know exactly what's wrong with you, 'cause, you see, I've been having the same symptoms myself. Can't eat, can't sleep, can't do much of anything. Go through the days, one after the other, kinda like a zombie on autopilot."

The laugh that broke from her was more sob than chortle. The description was so accurate of the life she'd been leading the past month she wanted to yell, "*Bullseye.*"

"I think I know what can make us both better."

Without a word, he took one of her trembling hands, and then gently tugged on her arm, forcing her to stand. When she was, his uninjured arm effortlessly slid around her waist, under the jacket. Ignoring the curious stares around them, Cal pulled Silvestra close.

"Cal-"

"Shush, darlin'. Take your medicine like a good girl."

His mouth barely scraped over hers, and yet Silvestra felt like every nerve in her body had been set on fire. Gently, like a butterfly's wings flapping against her skin, Cal traveled across her mouth, her chin, the line of her jaw. They could have been totally alone for all either cared about the people milling around them.

"I've missed you so much, Silvestra," he whispered into her hair, trailing kisses across it. "Tell me you've missed me, too."

On a sigh that came up from her toes, Silvestra did. "I have. So much. But-"

Cal smiled into her hair. "No buts. I told you that once before, and I meant it." He pulled back a fraction, stared into her eyes. "You left because you told me you couldn't stand the pain that loving me, being with me, might bring. Remember?"

"Yes."

"My guess is this past month you've been in as much pain as I've been, right?"

It was true. She told him so.

"Well now," he pulled further back, eyebrows arched, and said, "If we're both in so much pain apart, and you think you'll be in pain when we're together, why don't we share our misery? Seems to me it'd be more fun to be together, miserable, than separated."

It took her a moment to understand. When the dawn finally broke, she burst out laughing. "That's the most convoluted logic I've ever heard, Sheriff. And the weirdest."

His grin was wicked and deadly. "Yeah, but is it weird enough to convince you to marry me?"

Her laughter died. "What?"

His grip tightened. "Silvestra Coeltrain, I love you. I have since that first day. I can't explain it, but we complete each other. You've been as wretched as I've been the last few weeks, and the reason is plain as day."

Cal's eyes raked across her face. "I love you," he said. "Marry me. Build a life with me. I've waited for you my whole life. I can't and won't let you go. I did before and I was wrong to. I know now I should have done everything in my power, including throwing you in a jail cell, if that's what it would have taken to prevent you from leaving."

She was silent for a moment. Then, "A jail cell?"

"If I'd thought of it, believe me, I would have."

The thought sent an unexpected shiver of desire down her spine.

"I'm not going back to Renewal without you," he said, the firmness underscoring his conviction. "What d'ya say, Silvestra? Will you marry me, take a chance, make a life with me?"

Could she? She knew now a life with him was what she wanted. If the past month had taught her one thing, it was she was miserable without him. Even his twisted logic had a spark of truth. Why not be together? Why not take the chance?

Silvestra loved him, more than she ever thought possible. Seeing him again confirmed it.

When she smiled and nodded he let out a huge sigh heavy with relief. He picked her up, one-handed, and spun her around the aisle, whopping.

The sound of clapping and cheers stopped him. Looking up, he saw his nieces leaning over the cafe railing, applauding and yelling their happiness. They weren't the only ones. At least a dozen customers milling about the bookstore had been privy to his proposal. They, too, showed their delight at her answer.

When he let her go, he leaned back, a serious look on his face.

"What?" she asked.

"There is one thing you have to promise me before we get married."

When both eyebrows rose, he answered the silent question. "You have to teach me how you weave your magic with a fishing rod. That's my only requirement pre-nuptially. Promise?"

Silvestra threw herself into his arms and held on for dear life. "I promise." Gleefully, she pulled back. "But it's not easy. You'll need a lot of lessons."

His smile knocked the wind from her. "That's what I'm counting on," he said, grabbing her back for another kiss. Before his lips came down to hers, he added, "A lifetime of lessons."

Acknowledgments

First I have to thank the readers who plunked down their hard-earned cash (especially in this day and age) to read this book and any/all of my other stories. Without your love and support I wouldn't be able to write, so thank you from the bottom of my heart.

Writing is such a lonely, solitary endeavor. The only company you really have are your characters. To that end, I want to thank a few people for their unending support, wisdom, and for always being there when I have a ridiculous question or concern.

First, fellow writer and friend, Kari Lemor. Kari was the one who introduced me to my new formatting program and once I got the hang of it I never looked back. This makes being an independent author *sosososos* much easier and that means I can spend more time writing than formatting and everything else.

To Clair Brett, current President of RWA and dear friend. Clair is my writing accountability coach and believe me – she takes her job seriously! Because of her I always make sure I get my minimum of 1000 words in, daily.

Finally to my family and dearest friends. Your love, support, and encouragement have made these past 6 years of my writing career so worthwhile that I have no words other than I love you all and thank you.

I hope you enjoyed Cal and Silvestra's story. Look for the next in the Welcome to Renewal series, coming in 2023, **The Rancher meets his Match.**

About Author

Peggy Jaeger is a contemporary romance writer who writes Romantic Comedies about strong women, the families who support them, and the men who can't live without them. If she can make you cry on one page and bring you out of tears rolling with laughter the next, she's done her job as a writer.

Family and food play huge roles in Peggy's stories because she believes there is nothing that holds a family structure together like sharing a meal...or two...or ten. Dotted with humor and characters that are as real as they are loving, she brings all topics of daily life into her stories: life, death, sibling rivalry, illness, and the desire for everyone to find their own happily ever after. Growing up the only child of divorced parents she longed for sisters, brothers, and a family that vowed to stick together no matter what came their way. Through her books, she's created the families she wanted as that lonely child.

When she's not writing Peggy is usually painting, crafting, scrapbooking, or decoupaging old steamer trunks she finds at rummage stores and garage sales.

As a lifelong diarist, she caught the blogging bug early on, and you can visit her at peggyjaeger.com where she blogs daily about life, writing, and stuff that makes her go "What??!"

Visit her on her Website: http://peggyjaeger.com/

Also By Peggy Jaeger

<u>The MacQuire Women</u>
Skater's Waltz
There's No Place Like Home
First Impressions
The Voices of Angels
Passion's Palette

<u>Will Cook For Love</u>
Cooking with Kandy
A Shot at Love
Can't Stand the Heat

<u>A Pride of Brothers</u>
Rick
Aiden
Dylan (TBA)

Theo (TBA)

<u>The San Valentino Family</u>
3 Wishes (A Candy Hearts Romance)
A Kiss Under the Christmas Lights
Christmas & Cannolis
Mistletoe, Mobsters, & Mozzarella

<u>NYC Socialites</u>
Dirty Damsels (Dot Com Girls)
It's a Trust thing
Woke
Balance
Influence (2023)

<u>A Match Made in Heaven</u>
Dearly Beloved
Yesterday, Today, Tomorrow
Baked with Love

<u>Heaven's Matchmaker</u>
Mix and Match
Love match (TBA)
Perfect Match (TBA)
You're my match (TBA)

Hope's Dream (Deerbourne Inn)
Vanilla with a Twist (One Scoop or Two)

<u>Romantic Hauntings</u>
Merry's Ghost
The Haunting of Wilton June (2022)

<u>A Dickens Romance</u>
Angel Kisses and Holiday Wishes
Santa Baby
Fixing Christmas
Sasha's Secret Santa (2022)
Don't Mess with the Mistletoe (2023)

<u>Welcome to Renewal Series</u>
The Sheriff and the Psychic (2022)
The Rancher Meets His Match (TBA)
To Tame a Wild Stallion (TBA)